More Praise for *Making Love*

"From a Japanese internment camp to the rural Midwest, Fearnside moves his diverse characters with effortless prose through issues of racism, abuse, religion, and loneliness. These are characters desperate to fight against the earth's final pull, refusing to be buried, cut down, or to suffer temptations that will keep them from their final reward. Fearnside's compassion and unique vision shines over and within these questioning souls."
　　　　　—Tara L. Masih, Series Editor, *The Best Small Fictions*

"Jeff Fearnside is a master of moments that lift his characters beyond the humdrum into haunting realms of fear and ecstasy. His titular story is a moving exploration of sexual intimacy, its terrors and joys. In another, a farmer's desire to feel the 'renegade bluestem and slough-grass brushing his fingertips' tempts him to flee a cultivated landscape. The innovative 'Going for Broke' interweaves a young man's history in World War Two Japanese-American internment camps with moments after the war when he's pitching a no-hitter, the game of his life. In Fearnside's brilliant 'Maps and Compasses,' a young man sharing his survival with a buck sees in the wild animal's eyes 'a greater life' than he has ever seen. Read these stories! Flight by flight, they break above clouds of the everyday into moments of jaw-dropping wonder and clarity."
　　　　　—Wendell Mayo, author of *The Cucumber King of Kédainia: Fictions*

"In his debut collection, *Making Love While Levitating Three Feet in the Air*, Jeff Fearnside has written authentic and moving stories that explore love and complex relationships. Indeed, Fearnside's narrators take the air by storm and generously swoop through thematic layers in their investigation of fathers and sons, lovers, friends, hunters, surreal cat-like aliens, even Japanese internment camp residents. In these remarkable tales, the reader finds sure footing in the humanness of such disparate individuals, but by the end of the book, we, too, have taken wing in a beautiful flight of fancy, understanding life's little defeats and victories. This book will inspire!"
　　　　　—Cate McGowan, author of *True Places Never Are*

"Fearnside's prose is succulent with sensory detail. Through the lens of his characters' lives, he offers a keen awareness of history and human experience in all its spiritual, emotional, and physical complexity. Whether a character is scooping his hands into the sandy loam of earth on a farm or playing baseball inside a Japanese internment camp, we feel the depth and complexity of people whose lives might otherwise go unnoticed. Fearnside's imaginative accounts render the world both real and beautiful in a way that celebrates ordinary humans whose acquaintance you'll be glad to make."
—Lisa Norris, author of *Women Who Sleep with Animals*

"Like an airplane lifting off the tarmac at dawn, these stories amaze with their power and their seeming simplicity. At turns humorous and profoundly compassionate, they illuminate the lives of ordinary people—a baggage handler, a housewife-turned-editor, a farm boy—showing them to be both exceptional and universal. Here is a collection that challenges us to see in others what we may only dimly sense in ourselves, the humble beauty of the human struggle, its immediacy and its complexity. And while Fearnside brings forth a masterpiece of insight, he does so with such a light touch, the reader might easily be lured into thinking they were overhearing a conversation spoken by a campfire or in the halls of a country church, not realizing that Fearnside has translated into words the dialogue of the heart."
—Karelia Stetz-Waters, author of *Forgive Me If I've Told You This Before* and *Something True*

"Each and every story in Jeff Fearnside's debut collection is a new exploration into human need, depravity, tenderness, and ineptitude, a combination that Fearnside employs with the skill of a master. It's a book that's teeming with sex and nostalgia, anxiety and elation, highlighting what we're all capable of, to what lengths we'll extend ourselves to make things just a little better. It feels more like a tenth book than a first, this wise writer so in tune with humanness, it's clear he's been doing it, living it, his entire life."
—Mike Czyzniejewski, author of *I Will Love You for the Rest of My Life: Breakup Stories*

MAKING LOVE
WHILE LEVITATING THREE FEET
IN THE AIR

MAKING LOVE
WHILE LEVITATING THREE FEET
IN THE AIR

and other stories of flight

JEFF FEARNSIDE

STEPHEN F. AUSTIN STATE UNIVERSITY PRESS

For more information:
Stephen F. Austin State University Press
P.O. Box 13007 SFA Station
Nacogdoches, Texas 75962
sfapress@sfasu.edu
www.sfasu.edu/sfapress

Book design: Shaina Hawkins
Cover design: Shaina Hawkins
Distributed by Texas A&M University Press and Texas Book Consortium
www.tamupress.com

LIBRARY OF CONGRESS CATALOGING-IN-PUBLICATION DATA
Fearnside, Jeff
Making Love While Levitating Three Feet in the Air, and Other Stories of Flight/
Jeff Fearnside

ISBN: 978-1-62288-103-1

Who shall declare the joy of the running!
Who shall tell of the pleasures of flight!
—Amy Lowell

flight[1] *n. 1. The act or process of flying. 2. A swift passage or movement. 3. A scheduled airline trip. 4. A group, esp. of birds or aircraft, flying together. 5. An exuberant or transcendent effort or display:* a flight of the imagination....

flight[2] *n. An act of running away.*
—The American Heritage Dictionary

CONTENTS

ACKNOWLEDGEMENTS

The author gratefully acknowledges the following journals in which the stories in this collection first appeared.

"Nuclear Toughskins" first appeared in *Many Mountains Moving.*

"Clean" first appeared in *Controlled Burn.*

"Every Living Thing That Moves" first appeared in *Isotope: A Journal of Literary Nature and Science Writing.*

"A Story of My Very Own" first appeared in *Cantaraville.*

"Stars" first appeared in *The SFWP Quarterly.*

"Maps and Compasses" first appeared in *Homestead Review.*

"She Was a Winter" first appeared in *Eureka Literary Magazine.*

"Making Love While Levitating Three Feet in the Air" first appeared in *The Pinch.*

"Little Murders" first appeared in *Rosebud.*

"Going for Broke" first appeared in *Scent of Cedars: Promising Writers of the Pacific Northwest.*

"The Cat People" first appeared in *Fjords Review.*

"The Great Silver Cactus of Driggs, Idaho" first appeared in *Lake Effect.*

"Wing Walking" first appeared in *Arroyo Literary Review.*

The author also thanks *Many Mountains Moving* for awarding "Nuclear Toughskins" First Place in its 2005 Flash Fiction Contest; the Santa Fe Writers Project for awarding a portion of this manuscript (the first five stories) a Grand Prize in its 2005 Literary Awards Program; the New Rivers Press for honoring the entire manuscript in a slightly different configuration as a finalist in the 2009 MVP Competition; and *Permafrost/* University of Alaska Press for honoring it as a finalist for the 2015 Permafrost Book Prize in Fiction.

NUCLEAR TOUGHSKINS

My dad built a bomb shelter in our backyard the year I was born, between the Berlin Wall and the Cuban Missile Crisis, but it soon became a neglected cave of concrete and canned peaches over which my best friend Johnny Lynn and I ran barefoot and ice-cream sticky on hot summer days, or stalked fireflies at night, or threw our heads back and stalked stars, my dad standing over us tracing the flight of what we couldn't see, saying, *They're up there, boys, looking down on us as we speak, that's why it's a race to the moon, everything's a race.* Then muttering *godless heathens* he'd light a Salem and suddenly say, *Wave to them hi!* and we'd all wave except Johnny Lynn, who'd give the Reds the bird, though you couldn't tell, he was so tan and his gesture just part of the night. My arms were tan, too, but my legs were as pale as the powdered milk my mom would sneak from our cave when we ran out of whole, because no one in our family wore shorts, it wasn't allowed, something in the Bible supported this—Sodom and Gomorra, I was led to believe. But Johnny Lynn went to the same church as we did and was as dark as an Indian from the thighs down, and my parents never said he was going to hell, though I knew he swore and gave the Reds the bird and old Mr. Franklin, too, at the five and dime, not because I ever saw it but because my friend said so. I wanted Indian thighs and grass-stained knees but was afraid I'd be turned into a pillar of salt or destroyed by fire. Not even Armstrong's one small step could change my fear—it took the three channels on our TV, Mark Spitz and his seven golds, the forbidden rock on my transistor radio, and Skylab, which I imagined was manned by Major Tom, and by the summer I was twelve I couldn't wait to take my protein pills and put my helmet on, so one day I cut up a brand-new pair of Toughskins jeans. It wasn't easy because new was when they were best, like Dacron armor, but I figured if you could make a trampoline out of them, then they would make good shorts. The only thing is, I couldn't cut them with my school scissors or even my Scout knife; I had to sneak my mom's sewing scissors out of her basket, and I still had a hard time, especially with the reinforced knees, but when I was finished they were even cooler than Johnny Lynn's. And for one glorious afternoon, I ran with the freedom of one who lived free, who felt the heat of sunburned shinbones yet also impossible light and air rustling through downy hair like a breeze through curtains before a thunderstorm, ran as an equal with my friend. We danced and taunted the sky where we knew Salyut lay hidden godless behind clouds, *Look, Reds, look at us, see how we live in America!* until my mom heard and chased Johnny Lynn away before scolding me inside and stripping me to my briefs, fretting about what to do with my sin. She didn't tell me to wait until my father got home like she usually did but instead scolded and fretted and then finally made me dig a hole in the garden, where she deposited my new Toughskins shorts like they were a full diaper, covered them up, and said not to tell my father unless I wanted a red bottom.

They're buried there still, I guarantee it, have outlasted Vietnam, the Olympic boycott, the Cold War, Star Wars. They were probably just getting broken in when the Berlin Wall fell. Someday somebody will dig them up, long after we've finished the arms race and visited Mars, long after perestroika, the Second Coming, the two-thousand-year reign of the Prince of Peace my mom still says is right around the corner.

CLEAN

Walking into the humid, brightly lit Laundromat, he hardly noticed that the woman standing by the row of dryers was naked. They were the only two people in the place, but he was already thinking ahead to joining his friends, drinking and laughing and enjoying the clear April evening. He loaded his clothes into a washer, inserted four quarters, and closed the lid. He liked to pour his detergent in after the machine had filled up; his clothes, he felt, came out cleaner that way. While waiting, he sat in a molded plastic chair by the windows, where he found a copy of *Sports Illustrated.*

It was last year's swimsuit issue. He thumbed through the dog-eared pages quickly, skipping over the cover feature and news on what he considered minor sports until coming to an article detailing another baseball labor dispute. When his machine stopped filling, he stood and passed the naked woman sorting her dry clothes. He absently noted that she looked about his age, twenty-five, though she could have been twenty or thirty. He measured out a capful of liquid detergent into his washer, as the bottle directed, then added another half a cap, as the suggested amount was never enough. As he walked back to his seat, she was wriggling into her panties. He plopped down and picked up the story where he had left it.

A few minutes later, he slapped the magazine upon the scattered pile beside him and stretched. He had already forgotten about the woman, and her voice startled him.

"Would you please help me with this?"

Her arms behind her back, she appeared to be struggling with something. He stood again and approached her.

"The clasp is broken," she said, turning so that he could hook her bra. It was a little tricky. He fumbled with it, laughing to cover his embarrassment. When he was done, she spun back around and smiled at him.

"Thanks," she said and then returned her attention to her pile of clothes.

Uninterested in more outdated news, he paced up and down the Laundromat. The air felt tropical—redolent with detergent, lint, and mold from an opalescent puddle on the concrete floor—but it was as bright as an operating room inside, the reflection of the fluorescent interior sharply focused in the windows against the darkness outside. The whole establishment shimmered there on the glass: the row of dryers behind him, the two rows of back-to-back washing machines in front, and to his right, by a large table near where he had sat, the woman. She had picked out a pair of socks or stockings and was pulling them on.

His washing machine began clanging boisterously, and he tapped out a sympathetic rhythm on its lid. Boom, boom-boom, BOOM. Boom, boom-boom, BOOM. When he glanced at the windows again, she was pulling on her jeans, worn and slightly baggy. The window sash cut off her reflection mid-calf, and he couldn't see her socks. Or were they stockings? Suddenly he wished he had been paying more attention. What kind of woman was she—earthy ragg wool, sporty cotton, or practical poly-cotton blend? Maybe she preferred playful knee-highs. There was even an outside chance she wore thigh-highs under her jeans for the secret pleasure of feeling sexy it gave her, even if no one else knew.

He snapped out of his thoughts to find her buttoning up a plain white blouse. It stood in stark contrast to her skin, which he now noticed was tanned. But it didn't appear to be a "fake and bake," something bought at a tanning salon. How had she managed to hold on to the sunlight over the long winter? He looked at his own pale arms and decided he had to get out more.

When she pulled on a large cotton sweater, he abruptly stopped drumming. Though he was barely able to discern her shape through her blouse and the loose knit of her sweater—a slight peak here, a shadowed curve there—he felt as if he were seeing her for the first time. A vague aggressiveness stirred in him, competing with an equally vague sense of restraint; he wanted to see more, but without it appearing obvious. Under the pretense of sitting back down and reading another magazine, he approached her again, though more slowly than before.

He passed her as she was tying her shoes. Out the corner of his eye, they looked like tennis shoes, but he didn't dare look down. Instead, he walked more quickly to his seat and grabbed the first magazine he saw, a nine-month-old *Cosmopolitan*, which he pretended to read while watching the woman continue to dress.

She was now pulling a braided leather belt through the loops in her jeans. From her casual style, she could have been almost anybody. Was she an athlete, with the compact muscles of a mountain biker or long ones of a runner? Or was she a bookworm more used to exercising her mind, with softer, perhaps more delicate legs she liked to pull up under her and the covers on cool nights like tonight, a hot mug of tea steaming nearby? Did she have lean hips, hard to the touch like something sculpted, or fleshy ones, with skin soft as petals? He was almost desperate to know—he couldn't remember—but she had already fastened her belt, tucked in her blouse, and pulled down her sweater, which hung formlessly about her thighs. When she turned to check the clock behind her, the sweater pulled up more tightly against her for only a second before falling back like the rustling folds of a stage curtain suddenly dropped.

She then quickly pulled her hair into a loose ponytail, two stray strands hanging long on either side of her face. Now he felt he had some sense of who she was—a painter or poet, perhaps, her hairstyle reflective of a certain maverick attitude only lightly stayed by a civilizing hand. But in the next moment she put on a baseball cap, and the effect was completely changed. Was she a sports fan? Or did she simply enjoy the flexibility wearing such a cap gave her in styling or not styling her hair?

He studied her face more deeply to discover some clue to her personality, some habitual action that had marked itself in her flesh. Her face, though impassive, appeared kind. He looked closer. Her lips were relaxed but not exaggeratedly pouty, not self-consciously full. Yes, it was there, a natural history of her laughter and smiles in the turned-up corners of her mouth. Her eyes were soft and deep, accented by subtle but distinct purple creases. He wondered what had caused them, what obligations or late nights. Was she a student, a businesswoman, a mother? She pulled a pair of glasses from a case and put them on, and her eyes became indistinct behind the lenses. From her purse, she traded the case for an apple.

Finally, slowly, with the kind of grace impossible to practice, and which, being uncontrived, was all the more alluring, she pulled on a pair of tight leather gloves. She closed her purse. She was ready to go.

He had never seen a more desirable woman than the one walking toward him now, purse slung casually over one shoulder, fully clothed. A raw, sweet scent cut cleanly through the green-house air and its complex perfume of detergent, lint, and mold. Something possessive, fully aggressive rose in him, though he only dimly felt this in the rush of other feelings that automatically directed his actions. He couldn't let her leave without at least learning her name. As she was passing, he stood and said the first thing that came to his mind.

"Excuse me, can I borrow some of your detergent?"

She cocked her head quizzically, turned, and looked at the bottle still sitting by his washing machine. He thought quickly.

"I like my clothes extra clean."

She laughed, her eyes wrinkling at the corners, and then continued toward the door. He called after her to wait, asked what her name was. She didn't stop this time but laughed again, tossing her fruit in the air and catching it.

"Anything. Anything but Eve, okay?" She walked out of the Laundromat. For a moment the cool spring air rushed at him like water, carrying the mystery of leaves bursting from branches, the night a screen in front of which she was momentarily illuminated. When the door swung shut, he was left facing his own lone reflection.

EVERY LIVING THING THAT MOVES

In the gray early morning light, John watched his father squat and scoop his hands into the earth, pulling up a delicate shoot of corn. Chunks of sandy loam, unnoticed or ignored, dropped from his fingertips and onto his Sunday trousers. Around them, thin green blades flailed in the wind in rows stretching arrow-straight until crossed by the state highway a mile away. Above them, a thundercloud hung like the threat of violence. Another cold, wet spring had left mold on the corn stubble from the previous fall, and their seedbed hadn't had a chance to breathe; the new corn was at least two weeks behind in maturity. The bumper crops of the late eighties were only a couple of years past, but, as with most farmers, the difference between a good year and debt wasn't much, and John's father didn't take well to these kinds of setbacks.

I know what he's thinking, John thought, but I can't help it that it's rained so much—and anyway, I didn't make him try no-till this year, I only suggested it. He often wasn't sure what set his father off, or why, but the way his father held up the shoot, examined its spidery roots, and threw it to the ground told John all he needed to know.

Smacking his hands together, his father shook his head, his thin lips puckered tightly, eyes downcast. John quickly turned and began walking toward the small rise at the far end of this eighty-acre section, pretending to study the plants and soil. The air was thick with humidity. In his one good outfit, a light brown corduroy suit with a dark brown nylon tie, he began sweating, tense, imagining his father's eyes on him, waiting for the annoyed drawl, *John, I want you to come look at this.* He felt guilty for not caring more. As Cal and Irene Speck's only child, he knew he would own the family farm someday. But this was really his father's land, inherited from *his* father, a man rarely spoken of around the Speck household; the family history John grew up with centered around Cal only. It was made clear that he had paid for the land with his own sweat and blood for more years than John's sixteen by wrestling broken axles and untracked caterpillars, monkeying with wrenches as big as baseball bats, coaxing, prying, and pounding bright new machine parts in and rusted old parts out. He had plowed or combined long through the day in machines open to the heat and dust, and late into the night with the chill billowing through, had baled countless acres of straw and hay, loaded countless tons of grain onto semis, driven those semis for countless miles. John's grandfather had owned six hundred acres, passing on three hundred to each of his two sons. Cal now owned seven hundred and was always in the market for more. He'd never said so, but John sensed it made him proud that he would pass on more to his only son than all that his father before him had ever owned.

As John put more space between himself and his father, he relaxed, even felt lucky—the new season's planting had been enough to stir up the soil and possibly bring long-buried Indian relics to the surface. Ever since he had found his first arrowhead when he was six years old, his imagination had been fired by the history of his northwestern corner of Ohio. He had read everything he could about the land and its natives, and, despite the changes that had occurred, he could hear their stories now. The general flatness of the fields told of the glaciers that had repeatedly ground through between a million and ten thousand years ago. The intermittent sand ridges told of the succession of shallow lakes that had dammed up behind the last retreating glacier. The richness of the soil told of how these lakes had formed the Great Black Swamp, fifteen hundred square miles of tangled backwoods and sodden prairie, a special hunting ground to the Indians until white settlers began draining it more than a century and a half ago—a tale of men like his great-great-grandfather who had nailed together wooden troughs to funnel away the stagnant waters before the clay and then plastic tiles of succeeding generations. And the small, sandy hill John now approached, though slope-shouldered from years of being plowed, spoke to him again of an old Indian legend:

A chief named Tontogany once had a beautiful daughter who was pursued by a young man from another tribe. Chief Tontogany didn't approve of this man and prohibited his daughter from seeing him. But they rebelled, met in secret, and fell deeply in love. When the chief found out, he banished the young man to the prairie lands to the south. Knowing the punishment if he refused, the young man left, but his lover stole away to find him, and they said goodbye on top of a sandy hill overlooking the wet prairie. She stood there for a long time, watching him until he disappeared, and for days after returning home lay in a despondent state. Afterward, she often walked back to the hill to gaze far to the south until one night she never returned. Other members of her tribe later told of how she could be heard wailing on that spot a mournful song that echoed throughout the surrounding woods. The chief was so distraught, he forbade any of his people to visit the place. For many years it was still called Shut-nok by the white settlers, after the name of the Indian maiden.

Another version said that the chief knew his daughter had stolen away with her lover and had them followed, and when they came to the hill, the young man was killed. In 1879, workers excavating sand there did find the remains of a muscular Indian man buried with his legs to the east, a brass kettle between them, a rusting tomahawk and scalping knife at his side. He had a small, round hole in the back of his head.

Was it the wound of a disapproving father? Whatever happened to the daughter? John rarely tired of imagining that story and playing out its possibilities. Once, he'd found a smooth, triangular grinding stone close by, and he liked to think it had been Shutnok's, used to mash herbs or corn. The fine obsidian arrowhead he later found could have been her lover's, for killing wild turkey or deer. They would have fed each other that way.

As John walked, he saw a jagged shape lying in the sand in front of him. He eagerly bent down to pick it up, but in his fingers, the expected stone crumbled like old, brittle paper. It was a torn shred of cornstalk, withered to a deceptive point. A whoop floated over the field, and he looked back at his father, who was hollering and waving him in to church. John stayed down on his haunches a moment longer, soaking in the rot of the stubble around him.

John walked behind his parents along the unmarked edge of a two-lane road to the little evangelical church only a quarter mile east of their home. His father, an even six-footer, marched through the loose gravel on the road's shoulder, both hands in his trouser pockets, his head turned either to the fields or to the cloudy sky. His mother moved more carefully in the high heels she wore for her husband, a plain navy dress slightly snug on her medium frame. Along the way, they passed the parsonage and church cemetery where as a child John had often played "ghost in the graveyard," and which was still a favorite after-hours haunt for him and the pastor's daughter Sherry.

Every Sunday in decent weather the family walked like this, driving the short distance in snow and rain, but John had grown increasingly uncomfortable with the routine. He had always hated dressing up, though he'd resigned himself to that part, but now that he was older, church itself was a burden. Today was a communion day. Pastor Blount stood behind the wooden pulpit, looking out over the congregation with his thick-rimmed glasses at the end of his nose, a large man with a red, clean-shaven face and stringy black hair slicked straight back and falling around his collar. The pulpit couldn't hide his great, distended belly. He was the third pastor in the last five years at their church, and to John, they had all looked like old-time riverboat gamblers.

"Make no mistake about it, Jesus was sacrificed for us," Pastor Blount intoned, speaking in measured cadences that emphasized the hard consonants—mis*take*, sa*cr*ificed. He spoke of the repercussions of that act, of choosing to follow the truth of it, or of turning away from the truth. To emphasize the last, he read Acts 1:18–19. "Now this man bought a field with his wickedness; and falling headlong he burst open in the middle and all his bowels gushed out. And it became known to all the inhabitants of Jerusalem, so that the field was called in their language Akeldama, that is, Field of Blood." In Matthew's version of the story, the man—Judas—had felt so guilty, he hanged himself.

Everything comes at a price, John thought. But is that what Jesus was really trying to say? This was Wood County, Ohio. Its cities and villages were named after people who had lived, fought, and died there, both Indian and white—Perrysburg, Haskins, Tontogany. John could see Shut-nok's hill from his own house, the spot where her lover's blood had spilled. He could understand that sacrifice, the reason for it. But Jerusalem was so far away, and Akeldama sounded strange to his ears.

He looked at his family. To his left his mother sat with back straight and both feet on the floor, her hands folded in her lap, her face impassive. To his right, his father moved his tongue over his teeth and occasionally nodded his head.

After the service, the family filed down the aisle for the reception line in the large foyer where Pastor and Mrs. Blount shook hands or exchanged kisses with the members of their congregation. Their fifteen-year-old daughter Sherry commanded the center of the room, in animated discussion with a knot of teenage girls. John excused himself and stood to the side, where he pretended to wait for his parents in boredom. But, while he was careful to keep looking around, he always brought his eyes back to Sherry.

She wore a cream-colored sweater and a dark wool skirt that normally hung to mid-calf, but at some point, after leaving the parsonage she must have rolled the waistband over to raise the hem—a trick, she'd confided to John, to beat her father's inspections. Almost fully exposed, her calves ran in a straight line from her knees to her ankles; her arms looked like stray twigs sticking out of a bird's nest. She had a pretty face—a pale, clear complexion, dark sparrow's eyes—and long, straight brown hair held back by a plastic barrette. One of the other girls must have said something clever, because Sherry smiled, showing off large, evenly shaped teeth. John enjoyed spending time with her, as she lived so close by and went to the same high school, though she could become too chatty, too social, exhibiting a sexually charged flirtiness that she'd copied from the movies. But alone with him, she showed a seriousness and intelligence he liked. They could talk about things.

When Sherry's clique broke up, she walked over to him and said hi. He looked at the worn russet carpet and turned his head away from where his family was chatting with Pastor and Mrs. Blount.

"Hi," he said in a low voice.

"What are you doing tonight?"

"It's a school night. You know how my parents are."

She spoke more quietly. "I got some party favors."

He caught the inference in her raised eyebrows. "What time?" he asked.

"Near dark."

"I'll think of something." Just then his mother and father walked up.

"Well hello, Sherry," his father said. "Don't you look pretty today? Ain't she looking pretty, John?"

John didn't answer, and when his father slapped him on the back, he pitched forward slightly.

"Do you see how skinny she is?" his father asked. "That's how a girl should be. You can tell a good one by their ankles. If they have tiny ankles, then you know she'll still have nice legs after she gets older and puts on a few pounds."

His voice was loud, louder than it needed to be. Pastor and Mrs. Blount turned their heads for a moment and then quickly resumed smiling and shaking hands. John's mother didn't say anything.

A deep resentment burned in John. To embarrass him in front of other people was bad enough, but to humiliate his mother like that was intolerable. She was a beautiful woman. If there was anything wrong with her, he couldn't tell.

"Yeah, well I like a girl with a little meat on her bones," he said and regretted it as soon as the words were out. It made it sound as if he were agreeing that his mother was overweight. And it sounded like he was putting down Sherry. He wasn't trying to hurt her feelings. This wasn't about her. Without looking at anyone, he quickly walked away and pushed out the front door of the church.

At five o'clock, the family piled into the old Ford Galaxy 500 to look at surrounding farms. John sat in the back seat, Irene in front. Cal drove. Shortly after pulling out of their gravel drive, he popped open a can of Stroh's beer and lit a cigarette, and though he cracked the window for ventilation, all it did was blow smoke back into John's face. John had found that sitting in the middle helped some and also gave him better views of the countryside they cruised through, flat fields of corn, wheat, and soybeans, roads running square to theirs ticking by every mile, each with broad, muddy ditches alongside them filled with cattails, fleabane, horsetails, tiger lilies—while into the fields crept Canada thistle, sow thistle, and swamp milkweed. The saturated gold of the late afternoon light, the slanting shadows it cast over this landscape, depressed him today. He tried to think of something to break the silence, but he knew from the exaggerated way his father was sucking in smoke that words would come soon enough.

"That was quite a little scene you put up back there in church," his father finally said. "Care to fill us in on it?"

After a short pause, John said, "I wasn't feeling good."

"So you thought you'd embarrass your mother and me in front of Pastor Blount and his wife?"

"I guess I wasn't thinking."

"No, you weren't. Sometimes I wonder where your head is at." He fell silent, but John didn't relax. They drove for a short time, past the Underhills' wheat fields and one of Paine's horse pastures, but his father didn't say anything more until they passed another field owned by the Underhills, this one in corn.

"Field looks good this year," he said in an agreeable tone to his wife. "Looks like they did a nice job working it." He shifted in his seat and raised his voice again, pitching it back toward John. "And you sure weren't thinking too clear when you recommended going no-till, now were you?"

He had tried to remind his father before that Al Wilson, their hired hand, had really pushed for it after they'd put off using it for so long, but his father had it in his head that it was all John's doing because he had brought it up first.

"It worked good for the Skinners," he said.

"Well, it ain't working good for us. Did you see our corn? Or were you too busy daydreaming this morning?"

"I saw it." He hadn't wanted to see it, but he couldn't miss it. No-till worked great in drier weather, had been a boon to the Skinners and the Roots, who swore by it. It cost less in both money and labor and kept the land from blowing away in the winter. Rather than go over all of that again, John thought he would try a different approach.

"You know, though, I read—"

"I don't care what you read," his father interrupted, turning his head for a moment. "It's being practical that counts. Is this the kind of thinking they're teaching you in school nowadays?" When his father turned back around, John wiped a fleck of spittle off his cheek.

Little was said after that besides an occasional comment from his father on the rising price of land or falling price of grain. It's all about money, John thought. That's why he's so hacked off about the no-till; if we'd had a normal spring, he'd be taking all the credit. John understood that this land, his home, hadn't always been this way. He and his father had spent many long days burying drainage tile, miles of plastic packed like capillaries under the earth's skin, connected to a system of hundreds of miles of ditches, creeks, and rivers that constantly had to be dredged to keep them flowing free. It was hard work, the only way to keep the swamp from creeping back.

And God blessed them, and God said to them, "Be fruitful and multiply, and fill the earth and subdue it; and have dominion over the fish of the sea and over the birds of the air and over every living thing that moves upon the earth." John knew the Bible verse well, though he wasn't sure he believed it. Shut-nok's lover would never have drained this place. But men like John's father were only interested in progress, could only compare their fates to their fathers' before them. Hunting was better than it had been in years, the deer and pheasant fat and lazy on corn. Crop prices were down, but yields remained high. The problem wasn't the land, it was the damn government with its export quotas, grain tariffs, and farming subsidies that was gumming up the system. John could practically hear it in his head.

He looked at his mother. She had been staring out the side window for a long time, also apparently in thought. She didn't look forward, even when her husband spoke, though she occasionally nodded her head and hummed affirmatively. John watched his father take a long draft from his beer, heard the faint splash fall back into the can. Although he hadn't asked for a new one, John's mother suddenly bent forward and reached into the grocery sack sitting at her feet. She pulled out another can of Stroh's and popped it open. John's father drained his last swallow and, without looking at his wife, traded the empty for a full one. She carefully placed the can in the paper sack and resumed staring out the window.

John met Sherry at the cemetery as twilight fell softly around them, the color of a faded bruise. The cemetery sat on a sandy ridge set back from the road and surrounded by a rusty cast-iron fence, thick junipers, and budding maples. A large pile of sandy earth, left over from many years of burials, rose in the back, near an outhouse with crescent moons carved out on either side. John and Sherry sat cross-legged facing each other, the outhouse behind Sherry shielding her from the parsonage, the trees behind John blocking any view from the church. With the earthen pile between them and the road to John's right, they knew they couldn't be seen from that direction, the north, while only a field of corn, delicate budding shoots, watched them from the south.

Sherry opened a paper bag containing two sixteen-ounce Budweiser "tall boys." She handed one to John and then popped the top on her own and took a long swallow.

"Where'd you tell your parents you were going this time?" she asked.

"I told them I was taking a walk. I should be home in half an hour."

"Plenty of time." She took another long swallow and fell silent, the only sound that of beer falling back in the tipping cans. The evening breeze was warmer now, and John smelled rain. "My brother Robert says he almost got busted for his fake I.D.," Sherry said after a while. "We'd have to find someone else to buy us booze then. What about you? Do you think you could get away with it? You almost look old enough."

I've been faking my way through everything else, he thought, but resisted saying it out loud. Instead, he answered her question with one he'd been wondering himself. "When you get older—you know, after you graduate—do you know what you want to be?"

She started to respond quickly, as if she'd thought about it before, and then seemed to catch herself. "Oh, I don't know. Lots of things. A teacher, or maybe a doctor or a nurse. I like science. No matter what my daddy says, I'm good at it. But, I suppose mainly I want to find a nice boy and settle down, stay in one place for a while. It's hard being a..." Her voice trailed off.

She suddenly leaned forward and pressed her open mouth to his lips. Though he had daydreamed about something like this, he was surprised. Her mouth moved all over his, wetly, almost furiously, their teeth banging together a couple of times. She reached between his legs and rubbed his crotch through his jeans, where a deep, warm tingling rose up in him, but nothing else. Why wasn't he more excited? He felt overwhelmed. He tried pulling back, but she simply leaned forward further, moaning a low moan: soft yet fierce, insistent, the smell of beer heavy on her breath.

"This sure beats shaking hands in church, don't you think?" she murmured playfully into his ear, pulling at the top button of his shirt. He put his hands to her chest and gently pushed her to the ground, where she lay with arms spread behind her, legs apart. Instead of joining her, he turned and leaned against the earthen pile, cool against his back, while a flush of embarrassment filled his face. The feeling that things weren't in his control, the strong smell of beer, her comment—they all added up to remind him of something he had forgotten years ago.

Up until he was eight years old, he had always kissed his mother on the cheek and shaken his father's hand before going to bed each night. But one night, when his father had been drinking with two of his buddies, John kissed his mother lightly and then walked over to give his father's hand a quick squeeze. He held out his own hand, small, hairless, and pale next to his father's lying on his denimed thigh, holding a beer. His father looked up with a slight smile and glassy eyes.

"How come your mother gets a kiss and I don't? What about a kiss for your old man?"

His father's two friends chuckled and drank from their beers. His mother's head didn't move from where it was pointed at the television. John had seen other boys kiss their fathers, and no one seemed to think it was a strange notion now, but it didn't feel right to him. He was wearing his one-piece red pajamas with the feet sewn into them, and he felt ridiculous. He remained there with his hand out as if he hadn't heard.

"Your mother always gets a kiss. Does it seem fair that I don't? Haven't we always tried to be fair with you?"

Other boys kissed their fathers, he knew that, but he didn't want to. He was turning to walk away and just go to bed when his father spoke again:

"Give your old man a kiss."

He was still slightly smiling, but something sounded different in his voice. He didn't like being challenged. John leaned forward and pressed his lips dryly against his father's cheek. He smelled sweat and beery breath. The bristle of whiskers felt strange. He pulled back, nodded at his father's friends, and, without looking at his mother, quickly went to bed.

The worst part for John was that he had to take everything his father said as the law, or he ran the risk of looking like he hadn't been paying attention. So for a few days afterward he kissed his father on the cheek as part of what he thought was the new routine. The first couple of times his father said nothing, but it was clear he felt uncomfortable with what was going on and quickly brought back the handshake. Sitting next to Sherry by the pile of earth now, John suddenly realized his father hadn't remembered the next day what he had asked for. He probably had no idea what had caused the sudden display of affection in his son.

"What's wrong?" she asked, sitting up. "Didn't you like that?"

"I'm sorry. Spaced out for a minute."

"You're not drunk, are you?"

"No," he snorted, adding, "I guess I got a lot on my mind."

She appeared to consider his words. Even in the dwindling light, he could see her dark eyes gleaming, but he didn't know if it was from anger, booze, or unspent passion.

"Give it time," she said, gathering the loose strands of hair that had fallen from her barrette and clipping them back into place. "But not too much time. You should probably go home now anyway."

When John came in, his mother was busy in the kitchen, her back to him where she stood at the double sink, a stainless steel pot full of hard-boiled eggs on the counter to her left, peeled ones slowly filling a drainer next to a glazed clay crock on her right. The light over the sink gilded the stray wisps of graying hair falling from her bun. John had always thought his mother defined what a woman should be, with her height and quiet presence. Now he couldn't help remembering Sherry, her small breasts much firmer than he had expected when he pushed her away, her nipples, even through her sweater, pressing into his palms as insistently as her ribcage at his fingertips. His mother must have heard him enter, for turning her head only slightly she said, "John, could you do me a favor? You know how your father loves my pickled eggs, and I was just thinking how we *always* run out too soon. Could you run up to the attic and dig out that big crock we haven't used in so long?"

He looked at her kind face, smiling through tired lines, and then nodded and walked quickly upstairs, chewing harder on his stick of cinnamon gum in the hope it would cover up the smell of alcohol. He also didn't want her to see what the thought of Sherry was causing.

By the time he got to the attic, he had a hard-on. Mentally he kicked himself for blowing his chance with her, but it was too late now. He probably wouldn't get a second chance; girls like Sherry didn't make it with guys like him. He definitely couldn't go back downstairs as he was, so he tried, despite the stifling heat and dust, to cool his thoughts by concentrating on what he was looking for. The attic was the part of the old farmhouse that best showed its many alterations and additions. Wide planks with clearly visible saw marks ran the whole length of the floor, while timbers with the bark still on them supported the sloping roof from which two naked light bulbs hung at the ends of thick, frayed cords. In the broad space under the roof's peak sat a variety of trunks and boxes; against the walls were stacked pieces of chipped and unvarnished furniture, a clothes rack hung with faded clothing, and several metal shelves filled with junk. John even found a milk crate with his second- and third-grade notebooks in it. Why did his mother save all that stuff? Did she think he was going to use it again? That had been the idea behind keeping his seventh-grade science diorama, which was still set up on an old card table. After building it, he felt like he'd blown open the lid to a whole new world—a sustainable farm. It was a diversified operation with tempera-painted fields planted in specialty crops or vegetable produce rather than just cereal grains or soybeans, tiny cardboard milk cows ranging on grass, not tied to their feed boxes, and an aluminum-foil silo surrounded by matchbox trucks to show it was a cooperative venture. It had won first prize. When he had come home and held up the ribbon for his father to see, his father didn't reach out to take it and examine it more closely but simply glanced at it, grunting and nodding before returning to the newspaper. Looking at his farm now, John noticed glue showing where it shouldn't have and corners that didn't exactly match. The side facing the south window had been washed of all color.

He found the big crock sitting next to the card table. Inside were a pair of wooden badminton racquets, a folded canvas tarp, and what he initially thought was a small, framed picture. Pulling it out, he saw it was a college diploma for Benjamin P. Speck, 1938, Purdue University. John had never known his grandfather had gone to college. At the bottom of the crock was a leather-bound photo album, and John instantly remembered the last time he'd seen this, when he was six years old. He had always heard other people say what a spitting image he was, so he asked his mother what that meant, "spit an' image."

"Well, I don't know quite how to explain it." She laughed. "Here, let me show you." He liked how she acted when his father wasn't around, how she rummaged through the front closet without worrying about the noise she made. When she found the old leather album, they sat on the orange and yellow flowered couch and began flipping through the pictures. In all of them, his father wore genteel clothing—knickers and patent leathers, even a tiny tailored suit in some. In one such picture, he stood in front of an ivy-covered brick building that looked like a dormitory. Another showed his father and his Uncle Ray at the ages of two and four. Evidently his father's hair had been curly as a very young boy; in the picture those curls hung about his face, framing it like an angel's. Both he and Ray wore the same outfit, which looked like a cross between a sailor's suit and a dress, with wide collars, large buttons, and frilly ornamentation. It was strange to see his father without a plaid shirt and suspenders, even as a baby, and John laughed out loud at the thought.

They heard the back screen door slam, and his mother quietly took the album from his hands and closed it, but before she could reach the closet, his father was in the room. Without a word, he took the album from her and carried it into his den, where John heard a heavy thump on the desk. He had just stood up from the couch when his father returned and demanded, "Who told you that you could go rooting through other people's stuff? Your mother?"

"Leave him alone, Cal," his mother said, moving near them. "He's just a little boy."

"And he'll stay that way, the way you treat him. He needs to learn responsibility. Did you stop to think I might've put this away for a reason?"

"He was asking why people call him a spitting image of you. I just wanted to show him."

"Spittin' image! He doesn't seem to take a damn bit of interest in all the hard work I do around here, or even appreciate it. He never says a damn thing. Makes me wonder if we're raising an idiot."

"You can call me names all you want, but don't put down our son like that. I won't have it."

"You won't have it? *You* won't have it?" His father suddenly reached out and grabbed her hair from behind, pulling her head back so suddenly her mouth popped open. "I'm the man of this house, just like the Bible says it should be. A wife is to submit to her husband. I won't have you challenging me."

John lunged forward and hit his father on the fleshy part of his thigh. His father, with his free arm, shoved John back onto the couch so hard it bumped against the wall, slightly stunning him, but it wasn't pain that made him cry, it was shame and frustration—shame that he couldn't protect his mother or even himself, frustration that he didn't know how to. The whole time his father still held his mother's head, her neck taut, her vocal cords stretched.

For a moment John burned again with this remembrance, but he took a deep breath and thumbed to the back of the album, to the pictures he hadn't gotten a chance to see before. They ran until his father was about ten, and John saw no tractors or farm machinery of any kind, although there were some beautiful scenes of the country. It took him a moment to realize this was their property, before the east fence and buffer of swamp hardwoods—the elm, ash, oak, and hickory—had been cleared to make room for larger machinery. Feeling calmer, he closed the album, placed it carefully on the floor with the diploma, and then carried the crock downstairs to his mother, who was still peeling eggs. Since it was too big to fit in the sink, she asked him to wash it out for her with the hose, but he lingered.

"What was Grandpa Speck like?"

She stopped her work and turned to face him.

"Why do you ask?"

"Dad never talks about him. Nobody does."

She wiped her red, chapped hands on her apron and looked out the window over the sink, into the backyard lit bluish-white by the mercury vapor lamp on the side of the barn. She then leaned with the small of her back against the counter.

"You don't remember him?"

"I was only three when he died."

"Has it been that long? Of course, it has. Well," she drew in a breath that sounded like a sigh, "your grandpa was a big man, kind of built like a bear. He never had a mustache or a beard or anything like that; he always wore his hair short. Of course, that was the style back then. He was a farmer, but he was what you would call a 'gentleman farmer,' I guess. He worked the land a little, but he rented out most of what he owned. He made most of his money in the stock market."

John nodded. "Yeah, but what was he *like?*"

"He had a lot of friends. What did they *like* about him? He was witty. Yes, he was definitely that. He liked to host a lot of parties, barbecues and things like that. And he loved to read—novels, the Greek classics; he must've subscribed to every magazine there was. You would have liked that about him. And I think he would have liked the young man you've turned out to be.

"He could drink sometimes," she continued, talking more quickly now, "and toward the end, he didn't always keep a good eye on his money like he should have. When he died, about the only thing he had left that was worth anything was his land. Your father thought your grandpa was lazy. *I* don't think a college degree is impractical. It's just that some people are the way they are, and that's all there is to it. Your father's a country kid at heart."

When John asked what that meant, she replied that Cal thought his parents lived beyond their means, that they tried to be more than what they were, and that he wasn't comfortable growing up in the social circles he did.

"Is that why Dad never talks about them?" John asked.

His mother smoothed her hands on her apron again, lightly, turned back to the sink and began rinsing the peeled eggs under the faucet. "Your grandpa was really a sweet man," she said, her voice sounding hollow in the reflection off the porcelain sink. "He was. But he wasn't perfect. Something once happened between him and your father, when your father was just a little older than you, something he felt pushed into, I believe. Now, he would never *say* anything about it," she added quickly. "Guilt sometimes comes out in funny ways."

She stopped working for a moment, water splashing over the delicate, pale oval in her hand, and looked back at John. "You know, I really admired his attitude when we were in high school. He had that spark then."

༄

The back screen door creaked open and John's father entered the kitchen, wiping his hands on his brown Andersons overalls. He walked between his wife and son, opened the refrigerator, and grabbed a can of beer, snapping it open and gulping down half before speaking.

"Where were you?" he asked John.

"I was taking a walk like I told you. When I got back, I helped Mom find this old crock."

"You were gone a damn long time." He waited for John's response and then, when none came, blew up as if it were all perfectly clear. "I needed your help out in the barn! If I'd known you were going to take so long, I wouldn't have let you go."

The smell of beer was strong, so John tried to sound as casual as possible.

"On the way back I stopped and talked to Sherry," he said. "I didn't think it was a big deal."

"The preacher's daughter? What were you doing with her? Next time you say you're taking a walk, I want you to come right back, understand?"

"I thought you liked her."

His father got right up into his face. Beer, grease, and dust mixed with sweat and aftershave hung thick in the close space between them. Something metallic clattered into the sink. Out of the corner of his eye, John saw his mother grip the edge of the counter. His father's eyes gleamed.

"Don't talk back to me! What were you doing down there this time of night anyway?"

"I had some questions about homework." He was trying so hard to control his feelings, he began shaking.

"You know," disgust filled every slow word, "sometimes I wonder what you're learning nowadays. It sure ain't courtesy and common sense. You're always reading these books and coming up with these fancy ideas—you don't have any respect for the way things have been done around here since way before you were born. Do you think you're too good for us, huh? Got your head stuck up in the clouds? I think you've just got it stuck up your ass."

John felt the Black Swamp rise in him, something wild, something that wanted to reclaim what had been lost. He wanted to say, "Fuck you," to push his father away—no, to knock him to the floor, to knock that look off his face—but in his father's dilated eyes, John saw and understood two things: that this moment was exactly what his father had been pushing them toward for the past several days, and that if John jumped in now, his father was serious about teaching him some kind of a lesson. So John stood there, unable to act, not knowing if he was afraid or proud that he wouldn't play the game.

"Well?" his father said. When John still didn't respond, his father clenched his right fist, raised it, and shook it, his whole arm trembling. His mother was facing them, her mouth open as if to speak, but no sound came. "Ah, Christ," his father muttered, and without looking at his wife turned and walked into the living room, where John heard the sudden blast of the television followed by the rustling of a newspaper. His mother moved toward him with a towel still in her hand, but he brushed her away, knocking the towel to the floor. He grabbed his jacket and banged out of the house, leaving the screen door wide open.

John walked to the parsonage and knocked on the back door. Sherry answered, and when she saw who it was, she reached for a sweater on a hook by the door and called to her parents that she would be back in a few minutes. Taking John's hands she pulled him, running, into the gathering darkness and toward the cemetery.

They sat at their usual spot. A warm breeze carried the smell of wood smoke, lilacs, manure, and damp earth, the distant barking of dogs and more distant whine of semis driving through the night on the state highway. In the faint light, Sherry leaned forward, and he closed his eyes.

"I really like you," she whispered.

John opened his eyes, his mouth moving inarticulately in protest, trying to make sense of his feelings—she's lying, she must be lying, why would she like him? But she shushed him quiet, and as she leaned nearer, he smelled something about her, not a perfume, but something musky. Her breasts brushed against him and retreated, brushed against him again, pressed into him, and remained there. He realized he was holding his breath; her breath was also quiet, and he felt her heart beating rapidly against his. He could only see the outline of her thin body, a dark shadow against the slightly lighter shadow of the sky, as she softly pushed him back on the grass by the high mound of earth and straddled him.

Her mouth moved lightly against his. They fumbled with each other's shirts, then shoes, and then he pulled off her skirt while she undid his pants. He slid his hand under her panties, felt an oily moisture there, but when he tried to slide further he bumped into something.

"Oops," she said. "I'm on the rag." She pulled out a tampon and tossed it to the ground like a wet newspaper. He stuck his middle finger deep inside her, and the musky smell intensified as she wiggled around his finger and moaned, moving faster and faster, her hands pulling at his hair, his free hand stroking the taut skin over her hip, the smell of the earth around them seeming to well up in his head like the feeling in his groin.

After a few minutes she slowed, breathing heavily, and then slid off him and snuggled alongside him, her knees drawn up over his legs, her head on his chest. "I'm sorry," she said, hugging him tightly. "I told my parents I wouldn't be gone long." He hugged her back and stroked her straight brown hair, nuzzled his face into her neck and breathed deeply, breathed and wondered if her pillow smelled like that, of cinnamon and something else, something bodily but fresh, living. She lifted her head and kissed him, slowly, on his right nipple. "I don't want to leave. I want to stay here forever like this with you."

It took him a moment to realize he had stopped stroking her hair. She pulled back from him and began putting on her clothes.

"See you tomorrow?" she asked hopefully.

He hesitated, nodded, and then realized she probably couldn't see him from where she was standing. "Yes," he said.

"Yes?"

"Yes."

She reached out and squeezed his hand, letting it trail off her fingertips. He listened to her footsteps crunch down the gravel driveway and fade before slowly pulling himself up, putting on his shirt and shoes, and buttoning his pants. Through the screen of trees and shrubs, he saw a light on in the church and briefly thought of stopping there. Then he began walking home, taking the back way, along the edge of the cornfield. When he felt the soft boughs of the junipers that served as a windbreak, he knew he had reached his yard. Not wanting to go inside just yet, he stopped and squatted by the field. A few drops of rain pattered onto his collar, and in the distance, he heard the first groanings of thunder. It was completely dark now. He couldn't even see the outline of Shut-nok's hill.

Sherry's smell was on his fingers, and he dug them into the succulent earth. His parents would be wondering where he was soon, but when he stood up, he still felt like walking, out into the darkness to the south, into what once had been a forbidding and forbidden prairie. He imagined the renegade bluestem and slough-grass brushing his fingertips, his armpits, as he walked, and he wanted to keep walking, his footprints marking the path behind him only momentarily before filling up with ooze.

A Story of My Very Own

I guess you could say I'm the stereotypical good woman behind her good man. George writes stories—good stories—and provides a solid home by selling them to magazines such as *Field and Stream*, *Fly Fisherman*, *Guns and Ammo*, and once even to *Reader's Digest*, which really tickled my mother. I edit his stories, but I've never written one of my own.

Not that I'd want to. I'm not good with words, really, not like George. My mother used to wonder if I was good for anything, but George and I have a joint account, and the checks have always been in both of our names. He trusts me. He trusts me more than his old 486 laptop.

"How'd you get to be such a good speller?" he sometimes asks.

I smile and usually say something like, "Anyone can be a good speller when she has a spell-check program."

"But you catch things the spell-check can't," he always asserts, "like when I accidentally write 'there' instead of 'their.'" It sounded like he said the exact same word twice, but I knew what he meant.

George is my second husband. My first was a lawyer and very finicky; at first, I liked that about him—I called it his precision—but I grew tired of living up to his standards. It's possible he liked my cooking, how I kept the house, maybe even the way I made love. I don't know. Trying to communicate by telepathy wore me out after a while. George never wants salmon for dinner, and even if we had it, he'd never notice if it was overcooked. And he would never make certain demands of me in bed. He can fry lake perch over an open fire anytime he wants, often sleeps over bare rocks in the dead of winter, and finds my body beneath him a luxury he otherwise only dreams of at night.

That isn't to say we agree on everything. Like the other day, when I was reading over a piece destined for *Soldier of Fortune*, he asked, "Where'd you learn to write so good?"

"So *well*," I corrected.

"I would have caught that if I was writing—*were* writing."

"And I don't write well, I edit well," I continued. "Why are you asking?"

"Have you ever thought about writing something sometime? You know, a story of your own?" He raised his bushy eyebrows like he always does when he's excited about something.

"No, of course not, silly." I tried to sound playful, but the question annoyed me. Have I ever thought about writing something *sometime*? When did I ever have what that last word implied—some time? Between raising two boys, and volunteering at the library, and singing in the church choir, and shopping, and cooking, and cleaning, and editing George's stories, I can barely squeeze in my daily eight-block walk around the neighborhood.

But when I think of my mother, I still feel inadequate. She managed to do everything I do, it seems, but she never looked frazzled. I don't either—I have my woman's pride—but I've always felt frazzled inside.

"When are you going to be happy with the life God gave you,

sweetheart?" she always used to ask me. "A flower should grow where it's planted."

Once when I was feeling especially ornery, I shot back, "But you also say, 'Flowers don't grow in the shade.' What if I was planted in the shade?"

My heart was beating like it did when I later smoked my first cigarette. At this, my mother only smiled wider and said, "That's when you make your own sunshine."

In a funny way, she was right, though I didn't understand this until much later, after ten barren years, a bitter divorce, and then meeting the kind of man your mother said you never should, finding out that firearms *can* be used safely, and having two beautiful children and raising them up properly, which means teaching them how to carry a break-action shotgun with the barrel open so they don't shoot their feet off.

George once told me that some writers carry a tape recorder with them all day and record their every thought, just to make sure they don't forget anything important. Can you see me doing that? "Jonathan opened the peanut butter and then dropped it in aisle four, and I think the grocery stocker who came to clean it up had something he wanted to say." That young man actually flirted with me. He was sweeping up the peanut butter—Jif, so you know it was extra creamy—with a whisk broom. Can you imagine the mess he was making? At first, I was all apologies, but when I saw what a terrible job he was doing of it, I almost stopped and suggested that he bring out a pail and sponge. A little water and vinegar would have cleaned it right up. And while he's slapping away at this peanuty mud with his little broom, he's looking at my legs. He pretended he was talking to me, but instead of looking up, he looked to the side right at my legs. I would have been flattered if I were twenty years younger. I don't have much to offer anymore except a strong pair of eyes and seventy words a minute on the keyboard.

What am I saying? I was Phi Beta Kappa, a member of the Key Club, a soprano in the choir, and I *did* have nice legs. I even spent a semester in France as an exchange student, though my mother almost didn't let me go.

"Why do you want to travel to a foreign country when we've got so many beautiful places to see right here in America?" she asked, though she'd never seen any of them herself. I tried to explain that I wanted to visit the fairytale cathedrals I'd seen pictures of, but she sniffed and said, "We've got plenty of good churches right here in Maple Heights—*Protestant* churches."

She was right, of course, but have you ever seen a fairytale in the greater Cleveland area? Beer halls and bowling alleys, certainly, but there's a shortage of authentic medieval monuments. Now I wouldn't think of leaving my home. George and I live in Painesville, an hour east of the city. But back then, I was such a romantic young thing. I had my heart set on picture-book France, and eventually I talked my mother into letting me go.

I studied hard at the University of Toulouse, an ancient and truly wonderful institution deep in the south of France, but I also learned there was a lot to learn *outside* of classes. I met a young Frenchman who showed me a life I had never imagined before, couldn't have imagined. I tried smoking cigarettes, though only a few times, and got tipsy on wine more than a few times. Jean-Pierre even taught me how to properly pronounce a French "r," which no one in my high school, including my American French teacher, could do. I can still see the way he held his plum lips when he said it, two soft, plum moons.

And I saw my fairytale cathedrals. But you know what? The whole countryside was a fairytale. The land was so rugged and beautiful, with steep mountains topped with castles and lush valleys smothered in vineyards. It was nearly a paradise on earth, and Jean-Pierre told me that it had been once, back in the thirteenth century. It seems this group called the Cathars created prosperous collective villages all over the region at a time when the rest of Europe was living in feudal poverty. The Cathars were democratic before that was even a word. They translated the New Testament into common French so everybody could read it, and they believed women were equal to men. But the Catholic Church and certain rich nobles in the north didn't like this, so they started the Inquisition to put it down. When the Cathars were finally captured at Montsegur, some two hundred marched fearlessly down the mountain to a field, where they were burned alive while singing.

Singing.

I think about that sometimes when I feel tired or sad. My mother always said to whistle while you work. Singing while you die is quite another matter!

Now I'll admit, some of the ideas of these Cathars were rather strange. For example, while they believed in two creators—a good one, God, who created spirit, and a dark one, Satan, who created matter—they didn't believe in the Trinity. But they sounded like kind people. To burn them to death just because they believed God was one, not three? I don't understand that, though the idea of the Trinity makes sense to me. I'm three persons in one: mother, wife, daughter. Since my parents have passed away, you could substitute "editor" for "daughter." Or you could say I'm a mother, wife, and good woman. It doesn't matter.

If you think about it, Mary was the original good woman behind her good man. My pastor wouldn't like me saying this, but God the Father, the Son, and the Holy Ghost were just three lone hitchhikers standing around heaven waiting for a ride until Mary came along. She had the Creator of Us All to suckle at her breasts. Excuse me, but given the circumstances, I think it was perfectly acceptable to let the men build their mangers and herd their sheep and generally believe they were running things.

Even the young Frenchmen I knew, including Jean-Pierre.

"*Mon doré celui,*" he would say, for I had fair hair then before I snipped it and dyed it red, a special divorce present for myself, which I've kept. And instead of Elly, he always called me by my full name, Eleanor, which I prefer. "Why do you always say *non* and *une* when you could say *oui?*" He loved things like that, punning off the French word "yes" and how it sounds like the English "we."

Though he was a little cocky—I called it confidence then—he had a terrible crush on me. I liked him, too, but I kept thinking of my beau back home, and I wouldn't let Jean-Pierre and his plum lips touch me. If you only knew how twenty years can pass like a sigh… Then you would let more young men named Jean-Pierre touch you.

I could tell you more. I kept a journal the whole time, but it was awful stuff, really, this awful, dreamy, girlish stuff. At the time, it seemed so important, and I actually thought it was good. I know you'll laugh, but I even thought I had talent then—that I had potential, if I wanted to pursue it. Then one day after I had been back home for a while, I read it and was shocked at how mundane it all seemed. I wrote about my future first husband—a *lot* about him, how handsome he was, how strong and confident, how I couldn't live without him. Of all the guys on campus, I chose that slick-haired, smooth-talking law student. Asshole.

My goodness, I don't really mean that! Yes, I do. I just didn't mean to say it.

Of course, part of me wanted to stay, to travel through Europe that summer, but my mother wouldn't hear of it. "Someday you'll grow up and get married, too, and you'll realize I'm not full of horse feathers," she said. Marriage actually came sooner than both of us expected. Regret only came later.

I thought a lot about it, and I eventually decided that if those Cathars weren't afraid to leave France behind and march toward a new kind of life, then I shouldn't be either. After all, they had supposedly created heaven on earth, but it didn't last. That place that was a fairytale to me was where the Inquisition killed thousands. So I guess heavens are like flowers: you cut them down, and they grow again eventually. There's no need to go searching for them. Wait long enough, and they'll come to you. Don't tell my pastor I said that. But if those Cathars could sing while dying, then I could certainly live with regret. How's that for growing where you're planted?

Then I got a divorce and married George.

Now I can shoot a semi-automatic, filet lake perch no bigger than your hand, clean throw up from the back seat of a Dodge Caravan. Perhaps if I had known then what I know now, I would have done it differently, more kisses and more wine. But if I had a chance to do it differently now, I wouldn't. I can't imagine life without Jonathan and Trevor. And I love lying next to George at night. It's like sleeping next to a hibernating bear—he's just as immovable, nothing can wake him, and his snoring boasts complete faith in the coming spring. But I sleep very lightly, sometimes barely at all. Part of it has to do with being a mother. Even if George ever heard our children crying at night, his sleepy bear's body stumbling in the dark probably would just frighten them more.

But when the children are sound asleep, I still lie wide awake, listening to George's breathing, the radiator creaking in winter, the wind at the windows in spring, the crickets in summer and rustling leaves in fall, the house settling through every season. It sounds like poetry without words. I can't sleep because I don't want to miss what those things are trying to tell me. I can't sleep because I'm scared of what they might say.

Actually, my refrigerator makes this noise that even in winter sounds like crickets. It's at least twenty years old. The only reason we don't get rid of it is because it works. I know that's not fashionable in today's world—my friends all say I deserve a new Frigidaire—but I've never found one with a bigger vegetable crisper.

There's a metaphor in there, I'm sure, one that might be worth exploring if I ever wrote a story, a story of my very own. If I didn't love George so much, I'd slap him.

I once had this dream in which I learned how to shoot when my ex-husband became paranoid about the people he was prosecuting. I was standing behind him at a shooting range, patiently watching him fire away, when suddenly, for every nice thing he could have done but never did, I plugged him in his big round posterior. He yelped like a basset hound, but he wasn't really hurt, just scared. I ran up to him and said, "I'm sorry, I'm sorry," over and over again. "It was an accident." And he never suspected that it wasn't.

That's when my mother came to me. She was completely silent, but she had this faint smile on her lips just like she used to when my father would talk to company. She winked at me like we were co-conspirators in a secret plot, and I, remaining just as silent, gravely nodded back. I woke up then, and as soon as I did, I wanted to shout, "No!" Of course, I didn't. Still, for a long time afterward as I lay in bed, I felt a strange feeling in my throat, like I wanted to say something but didn't know what. I was actually a little frightened. The air wasn't chilly, but I had goosebumps all over my body.

Later, I understood what it meant. It was perfectly clear. Being a good girl isn't always a blind choice. It doesn't always mean turning your head away from who you are. Sometimes it means looking to become someone better than who you are. And failing. Then realizing that what you were aiming for was a mirage. No, not a mirage. A vision. A vision of another imperfect person who just happened to give you life and everything she knew about it. And when you realize that, you realize that living for someone else makes about as much sense as living for the past or for the future. Except for your children, who are the future.

It did give me an idea, though. The books I see on the "Suggested Reading" display at the library always have on their covers these ironic-looking young ladies with either too much makeup or not enough makeup, and the jackets talk about road trips and an endless stream of casual romances. Obviously written by those who don't know the first thing about cleaning throw up from upholstery. Or else they talk about these special, secret sisterhoods where the women can talk to each other about anything, and usually do. Do such things really exist? What I want to know is this: who's going to write a story about women who have few people to tell their deepest feelings too, who have husbands and ex-husbands and children, who have perfectly normal sex and like it? Women whose dreams don't always come true but who try to reach them, who make bad decisions along with good ones but at least make decisions? Women who aren't paralyzed by life.

STARS

S teve never meant to lose Linda in the forest. It was just that he was so excited to reach the high alpine lake that he ran up the mountain like a billy goat and left her behind. Once he turned to check on her while standing on the trunk of a massive Douglas fir that had uprooted over the trail, and she hadn't been more than twenty yards back. He then scrambled up a steep incline littered with scree and in five minutes turned to look again. At least it seemed like five minutes. She wasn't in sight, but as he was almost to the lake, he simply kept going and waited for her on a boulder by the edge of the clear water.

When another five minutes or so passed and she still hadn't arrived, he became worried and backtracked to find her about halfway up the steep section, where he offered her a hand. She pushed past him and after reaching the top fell against the nearest pine, gulping from her water bottle.

"You bastard!" she screamed when he tried to wrap an arm around her waist. She dropped the water bottle and beat at his chest. He tried to stop her, but she wrenched out of his grasp and turned away. At first, he thought she was laughing. Quickly, though, he realized she was crying, and only then did he understand what he had done.

"Why did you leave me?" she finally asked, her normally smooth, pale face blotched red.

"I didn't do it on purpose," he said.

"How could it not be on purpose? I don't understand how you can just go racing ahead like that."

"I thought you were right behind me."

"I lost the trail! And then I couldn't see you anymore, and I started calling, but you never came back."

Steve hadn't heard her calling. He must have been farther ahead than he had thought.

"Where did you get lost?" he asked.

"The trail stopped at that big log! It was too high to climb over with my pack on, but when I tried to go around, it was so dense in there, and, and…" She started crying again, and when she turned to him her pupils seemed entirely to fill her eyes. "It's just like you to do something like this. You're always doing something that shows you don't really care about me."

He knew she was talking about the upstairs neighbors again, and it irritated him that she would use a situation like this to bring it up. After all, he couldn't control what went on above them. But he felt so guilty about leaving her on the mountain that he resisted the urge to argue.

"I promise I'll always be there for you," he said. This time, she let him touch her, stroke the heat off her face. "I promise I'll never leave."

They pitched their two-person dome tent on the far side of the lake in a grassy flat near the head of an outlet stream, trickling low now that it was August. All winter long snow packed the surrounding bowl; they had discovered this by accident when as newcomers to Idaho they tried to hike this trail last October, only to find it blocked with drifts three feet high. But the beauty of the area had impressed them, and they had resolved to come back. By setting up so near the water now, away from the bowl's high granite walls, they enjoyed an unobstructed view of the sky. The lake mirrored the sunset's orange and aquamarine almost perfectly, though the occasional black fly or late feeding cutthroat disturbed the surface, bent the reflection in oscillating waves of light.

Best of all was the silence around them: no creaking floorboards, no mysterious thuds or shuddering bangs, only the swish of pines and snap of the tent's rain flap in the breeze.

Steve opened a can of beans and skewered two plump Italian sausages on a stick while Linda prepared a fire on a gravelly patch of earth. First, she dug a hole, which she rimmed with large rocks and filled with small twigs, then larger ones, and then finally well-seasoned deadwood they had scavenged from the forest. Despite the altitude, it took only two match strikes before the stack caught the flame. Linda looked pleased.

"Who says a *man* stole fire from the gods?" she asked.

While they waited for it to settle into a good cooking temperature, Steve opened a bottle of burgundy with the corkscrew on his Swiss Army knife and, after allowing the wine to breathe for a few minutes, filled two tin cups halfway, handing one to her and holding up his in the gesture of a toast.

"Here's to making it," he said. Afterward, he wasn't sure if he meant it as congratulations for scaling the mountain, as he had intended, or a prayer for the future. She hesitated and then drank without smiling.

A half-moon peeked over the ridge across the lake, astounding Steve with its brightness so early in the evening. Like Linda, he had grown up in Ohio, just west of Cleveland in Rocky River, and the hazy orange glow of city lights that hung over the night sky even in the suburbs obliterated most of the stars. But here in the Rocky Mountains, more than eight thousand feet up, miles from any other human, let alone a city, the moon and stars were brighter than he'd ever seen with his naked eyes. Not even the pulsing halo of the campfire could chase them away.

Something flashed overhead, a vapor trail of light, and then vanished.

"Did you see that?" he asked.

"Huh?" She was poking the fire with a moss-covered pine bough, watching the dried strands of vegetation contract in the heat.

"I just saw a firefly."

As a kid, he had captured lightning bugs in old peanut butter jars on countless humid summer nights. When he was a little older, he simply caught them and let them go, keeping track of the numbers, always pushing to set a new record. Later, he would lie on his back in the grass and watch the sky until his mom called him in. Then, pretending to go to bed, he would peer through his Sears catalog telescope at the stars winking on and off—the effect of swirling, invisible atmospherics.

"You saw a spark from the fire," Linda said, matching his excitement with dull evenness. "It was your mind playing tricks on you."

He shifted on the ground. "Why," he said, "are you always trying to tell me what I'm thinking?"

"How many fireflies have you seen since we moved here?"

"I suppose if I wait I'll get the answer."

"Zero. There aren't any fireflies out west."

As soon as she said it, he knew she was right. Because he hadn't seen one, it never occurred to him that he hadn't. "Well, why didn't you just tell me up front?" he asked, annoyed at his own ignorance. "Why did you have to beat around the bush?"

"I didn't do it on purpose," she said slowly, looking him right in the eyes.

❧

They had met three years ago at Peabody's Down Under, in the flats section of Cleveland by the Cuyahoga, the river that had caught on fire. He was finishing his law degree at Case Western Reserve University, she working as a receptionist in her father's oncologist's office. Clarence "Gatemouth" Brown was playing that night, and the club was full but not packed. Drinking a Rolling Rock out of the bottle at a side table, Steve was hypnotized by the tall woman with the swirling gypsy skirt out on the nearly empty dance floor, eyes closed, body swaying in a fluid, sensual manner. He liked that she didn't appear aggressive, desperate, like the women who danced here on rock and roll nights. He liked that she was there for the blues.

The lanky Brown put down his guitar and picked up his fiddle for a version of "Baby Take It Easy." Despite the switch to a more up-tempo tune, the young woman barely altered her rhythm, swaying at half-time to the music, her arms above her head like charmed snakes. Steve left his beer to join her, forcing himself to keep it slow, though he didn't feel comfortable with this, his eyes locked on her. Her eyes opened briefly, saw him, and then retreated behind closed lids, a slight smile warming her mouth. After Brown picked up his guitar again and launched into an old T-Bone Walker tune, she opened her eyes for good, watching Steve's. At the break, he offered to buy her a beer, and she let him order a Coke. He introduced himself and asked what her name was.

"Linda," she said. "Linda Dowling."

She was from Willoughby Hills, on the East Side of Cleveland, and they joked about the schism. The working class Poles, Slavs, and Hunks who made up the West Side looked at the East Siders with their urban brownstones and country homes as snobs, while the East Siders couldn't hide their pleasure in having the Museum District and grand Severance Hall on *their* bank of the Cuyahoga. The flats were where the two groups met and mingled. It was where Steve first touched Linda, on her cheek with the back of his hand; where, when he strayed near her mouth, she slowly closed her lips around his fingers and lightly bit them.

Steve held his hands toward the fire and then leaned back against the log behind him, taking another sip of wine.

"Aren't you going to cook our food?" Linda asked.

"The fire's not ready."

"I'm starving."

"If I put the sausages on now they'll just be burned on the outside and raw on the inside."

"I like them burned."

Steve took a long drink from his cup. "All right," he said, slowly pulling himself up and pouring the beans into his aluminum Boy Scout cooking pot, which he hung on a stand with a rotating arm that swung out over the fire. He then circled the yellow flames until he found a nook of amber coals, pulled his log closer to that spot, and sat back down, holding out the skewered sausages. Linda placed her mossy stick by the fire, rooted through her backpack until she found a can of cashews, which she popped open and began devouring.

The spice of sausages mixed with the sweetness of burning pine pitch, and Steve began growing hungry, too. The beans were nearly bubbling over. He swung the pot away from the heat, flipped the meat, and moved it closer to the fire. When it was done, he fitted each sausage into a bun and ladled the beans onto tin plates while she refilled their cups with wine. As soon as he handed her a plate, she took a bite of her sandwich and immediately began huffing in and out, her mouth wide open, moving the food around with her tongue. Before taking another bite, she forcefully blew on it, but still neither of them spoke. Steve looked up. The stars were streaked across the sky like jewels, a giant string of jewels that had broken open. That's what he eventually told Linda, just to restart the conversation.

She watched a spark kick up from the fire and sail dizzily away on the updraft before winking out of sight.

"Did you know fireflies are cannibals?" she asked, right before taking a big bite of beans. He waited for her to finish chewing and swallow. "Those flashes, the ones you *didn't* see earlier?" she continued, ignoring his sour look. "Only the females do that. It's an attraction thing, and it's also part of a caste system—so many blinks tells what caste they're in, so they can attract a mate from the same social order. Here's the wild part: sometimes when a female is really hungry, she'll blink the wrong number of times to attract a male from a different caste."

"So?"

"Then whammo! She eats him."

"And the moral of this story is?"

She set her plate down, and the ironic look on her face disappeared.

"The moral of this story is, don't let your female go hungry."

After a short pause, he laughed, genuine guffaws from the stomach. He set his own plate down and moved next to her, putting his arm around her shoulders and pulling her close, locking his free hand into one of hers. She placed her head on his chest and snuggled into his wool knit sweater, tucking her legs up under her and stroking his legs with her long fingers.

They had whiled away hours like this when they had first moved to Boise. Even though Steve had worked just as much then, it had seemed that he had more time—something about the freshness of being in a new place, of not feeling the accumulated pressures of the intervening year hanging over him. His volunteer work for the Sierra Club, the pro bono legal advice and hours spent maintaining hiking trails, was more than gratifying, it was necessary for maintaining a balance in his life. But he was beginning to miss the balance of her flesh.

They hadn't slept together the first night they met, hadn't

even gone home with each other. But Steve had remembered her name, the bold way she had announced it to him, a stranger in a club, and the next day he called to invite her for a coffee at the Arabica, the one in Lakewood, on the *West* Side. They made love a week later and were proud they had waited *that* long; both said they knew it was inevitable from the first night. Everything felt right, especially when they discovered early on that they each wanted to move west—west of the Mississippi west, the West of mythic mountains, craggy canyons, and wide-open deserts, a place to stir the blood and imagination, away from the East's thoughtless shopping malls and tangle of interstate highways like varicose veins.

Linda had wanted finally to put her environmental science degree from Oberlin to use. She fondly thought of her family's many ski vacations in Sun Valley, and after weighing her needs for culture and nature—nature winning—pitched the notion of Idaho to Steve.

"Why not? We can't even keep the most beloved home football team in America from leaving town," he had said, still angry at the loss of the original Browns. He would miss old Municipal Stadium and new Jacobs Field, the renovated downtown and historic neighborhoods, the good restaurants and even better music scene, but he looked forward to other possibilities. They did their research, and after Steve graduated from law school, studied for his bar exams, and passed, he soon found a job in Idaho's capital with a firm that handled the banking interests of such Western giants as Albertson's and Boise Cascade—not what he'd had in mind, but it would do for now. Linda cashed in on a tip from one of her father's Sun Valley connections and landed a job as an interpretive specialist with State Parks and Rec.

They were still in their late twenties, with no children and none on the way. They rented a turn-of-the-century apartment with twelve-foot-high ceilings, a brass chandelier, and hardwood floors, located near the trendy Co-op where they shopped. They bought a Jeep Cherokee and season's passes to ski at Bogus Basin, hiked and camped on the weekends whenever they could. Now they were looking to buy a house in the foothills. Somewhere in there they got engaged. They had become official Boise North Enders.

Still enmeshed with Linda by the fire, Steve groped for the bottle of burgundy, but it was empty, so he untangled himself from her to pull another bottle from his backpack and open it. This time, he didn't bother letting the wine breathe, just filled their tin cups to the rim. They both drank to make space before bringing their cups together in another toast, a dull tink followed by Linda's noisy sipping, interrupted when Steve began patting the air.

"Wait, wait, wait! It's your turn to make a toast."

"I'm no good at that kind of thing," she protested.

"You're supposed to take turns. That's the way it's done."

"Who says? You do it."

She fell silent, and Steve couldn't tell if she was waiting for him say something clever or trying to think of something herself. What would she say? *East is east, west is west, and never the twain shall meet.* He didn't know where that came from. *To new neighbors.* That was more her style. She held her cup in both hands as if to warm it, swirling the dark liquid inside.

"They're shooting stars!" he exclaimed.

"To shooting stars!" she said, lifting her head, then her cup. The jocularity in her voice held an edge of tipsiness.

He straightened his body and pointed his free arm to the blackness beyond the orange glow that surrounded them like an egg. "That thing I thought was a firefly earlier? It was a shooting star. I just saw another one."

"So there you have it," she said.

At the end of the lake, with the high granite cliffs spread

around him, Steve felt as if he were sitting in the end zone of Municipal Stadium, a cavernous, windy place that had bolstered the shores of Lake Erie before it was torn down, wide open to the sleet and swirling snow dismissed as "lake effects" by the locals, where anything could happen on any given weekend during football season. Only now the show wasn't just down on the field—the level lake—but up in the curvature of the sky. It fit snugly over the bowl like a bubble, reminding Steve of the planetarium he had visited as a schoolboy. But the stars were even brighter than those pin-dots of light that mechanically shifted and blinked as the planetarium simulated the changing seasons or points of view from the different hemispheres.

He had been working a lot lately. Two thousand billable hours a year. Who designed that system? That was forty billable hours a week alone. He had to work sixty real hours a week just to meet his quota. No doubt this put a strain on his relationship with Linda, but she was working, too—and anyway, they were going to need the money when they finally bought a house. They were well-off but hardly rich; he had student loans to pay, and housing in Boise wasn't cheap, not on the North End. For the most part, he liked his job. He only occasionally thought of his old Sears telescope and field trips to the planetarium, only briefly wondered if he wouldn't be better off teaching astronomy at some small college, where he imagined the sole pressure would be to publish a scholarly article every now and then.

But that was the kid in him still lying on his back in the grass, thinking of all that blackness between the lights—dark matter, the shadow stuff that makes up most of the universe. He took another swallow of wine. His face felt hot. He decided he must be sitting too close to the fire, so he scooted back, holding his cup away from his body to keep from spilling, which worked until he bumped into Linda.

"What are you doing?" she asked.

"I'm too hot."

"I think you're drunk."

"It takes one to know one," he said in a playful, sing-song voice.

A gust of wind shook the tent behind them and bent the frame diagonally, though the stakes held firm. Linda took off the scrunchy from her ponytail and shook her head, her straight brown hair swishing around her shoulders. When she stopped, wild strands of hair latticed her face.

Steve tried to drain the bottle of burgundy by adding more to each cup, and when they both couldn't hold another drop, he held the bottle up against the firelight, assessing it with one eye closed. He then tipped it to his mouth, finishing it off, before idly tossing it into the glowing embers.

"Hey!" Linda said sharply.

"I'm sorry. Did you want the last swallow?"

"I mean the bottle."

"I said I'm sorry. I should've asked you."

"Dig it out."

He drank enough from his cup so that he could set it down without spilling.

"What are you talking about?"

"It's going to explode if you leave it in there."

He looked toward the fire and finally understood what she meant. When he looked back to her, she was frozen, her eyebrows raised and shoulders slightly shrugged, both hands held up in her "There you have it" gesture. His only motion was to settle more comfortably against the log.

"I've never seen one do that," he said. "Besides, I like watching the glass melt." In the morning when it had cooled he would pick it from the ashes. He was a "pack in, pack out" kind of guy. She should know that.

She reached for the stick she'd been burning earlier and

tossed it onto Steve's lap. He picked it up and gently set it beside him, wiping motes of charcoal from his jeans while shaking his head. The wind must have loosened a tie on the rain flap because a free end now repeatedly smacked against the tent.

"If it bothers you that much, dig it out yourself," he said.

"Why should I always have to do everything?" She was suddenly furious. "Why can't you just be there for me for once?"

He breathed deeply, in and then out, trying to dispel the familiar sensation in the pit of his stomach, a tension, an acidic energy that put him on the defensive. "Aren't I here with you now? Aren't I here even though I have a pile of work waiting on my desk at the office?"

"That's my point. With you, it's always work, work, work, rush, rush, rush. Then you sleep like a peaceful, innocent baby all night long."

"It's not my fault I'm not as sensitive as you are." He held up a hand. "Yes, sensitive. You want me to toss and turn and worry and fret like you do, but I don't want to. I don't want to hear everything you do."

"No, you don't. That's the problem. Why would you want to see things from my point of view? Why should you actually have to work at a relationship?"

"They're just people, for crying out loud, people trying to live their lives. It's an old apartment, and we're not even going to be there much longer." He grunted and threw a pebble into the fire.

When they had first seen their apartment, they were charmed, but while they knew there would be the inevitable problems associated with an aging building, they never expected the seemingly indestructible claw-footed bathtub to leak or the beautiful maple floorboards to crack and squeak so much. They were early-to-bed, early-to-rise types. Steve slept like a rock, but Linda stayed up all night, listening to the upstairs neighbors walking all over them. The neighbors were a younger couple, in their late teens or early twenties, who worked evenings and kept odd hours. When they came home, Linda could chart their progress through the main front door, up the stairwell, and from room to room in their apartment. She had told Steve this and asked him to have a talk with them about it. He did, and then he came back and made his report.

"I don't know what to say, honey," he said. "They're aware of the situation and do the best they can. They even take off their shoes as soon as they're in the door."

"And you believed them?"

"Why shouldn't I believe them?"

"Because they're keeping me awake all night long."

"Honey, we can't expect the whole world to keep the same hours we do."

"It's like a herd of elephants above us."

The thing that got him the most was that she then began waking *him* in the middle of the night. The last time was last Thursday. He had been dreaming about work again—something about blowing up a couple thousand balloons so that his firm's main partner could pop them all at once for one of his clients—when she shoved him hard. For some reason, it fit with what was going on in the dream.

"It's the goddamned circus," she said.

"I'm going as fast as I can," he responded sleepily.

"It's about time." When he rolled over and began breathing deeply, she gave him another shove.

"Aren't you going to talk to them? You just said you would."

"The neighbors? I already did."

"And a lot of good it did! Steve, it's three in the fucking morning. They both get off work at midnight. What are they still doing up?"

"They need to wind down, for Christ's sake." He was awake and cranked up himself now. That ball in his stomach—it felt like somebody had punched him. "You know, I was asleep. Talk about being rude."

"They're making way more noise than two people who are supposedly trying to be quiet. What do they do, anyway? They're not in college, they're just working at some restaurant or bar—not that there's anything wrong with that if you're doing something else besides partying all night long. At least when you waited tables, you were working to get ahead in the world."

The rain flap was really beating the tent now, but Steve continued to stare into the fire. The flames were hypnotic. He felt he could see things in them. He loved Linda, but she was such a delicate thing, a ceramic figure that needed to be handled lightly. No, she was more like an opera diva, a strong, stubborn woman with nerves of glass who could shatter herself if she hit the wrong note. Who always had to be right. What would it be when they were married and living in their new home in the foothills—the sound of crickets? Flecks of wayward sand against the windows? The house itself settling around them?

"We'll find our own place soon, and this will all be over," he said quietly.

"You just don't get it," she said, her eyes dark chips of granite in a pale moon face. "This isn't about them. This isn't about them at all."

A gunshot erupted from the fire, and Steve felt something whiz by his head while chunks of flaming wood and a shower of smaller sparks blew into the air, a fountain suddenly and forcefully turned on, a terrifying and beautiful arc over them. He leaped to his feet with a yell. Linda was more precise.

"Jesus Christ!" she screamed, patting at her shirt while wildly looking around her. "Shit!"

Steve was numb. He watched Linda, still steadily swearing, jump toward the tent and begin brushing off smoky embers that were burning holes in the nylon shell. He knew he should join her, knew this was a hazard that needed his attention. But the explosion had blown the fire in a sunburst pattern from the pit she had built, and in the matted-down earth around it cinders glowed like stars fallen from the sky—scores of them, some glowing brightly, some dully, whole constellations flickering and sparking in the breeze. He couldn't resist entering this scene.

"I told you it would explode, I told you," Linda huffed, stopping her work briefly when she saw he wasn't putting out any fires. "Steve, what are you doing? Steve!"

He wasn't listening to her, didn't even turn around. In a moment he would. For now, he carefully moved through spiral galaxies, spidery nebulae, the dark matter between them.

Maps and Compasses

With his father's .243 Remington in the crook of his left arm, Ryan McAllister walked slowly through boot-high snow along the ridge's edge, looking down into the black-green mass of pines where he knew the old buck was hiding from the cold. He had read deer sign all along the way—the largest droppings he had ever seen, still moist, right on the trail where the buck must have emerged to eat the bunch grasses that poked through the snow like shocks of hair. Then there had been the prints, huge also, and the rubbings along the tall ponderosa a half mile back where the bark had been scraped away from the ground to six feet up the trunk.

The late-November sky shone a clear steel-blue above him, the air crisp and barely stirring. All around him, the forest stood silent under the small wintry sun except for occasional cascades of glittering snow from the firs and pines. More brush was exposed on the south side of the mountain, and Ryan would have been inclined to search over there except that the weather had been fiercely cold for the entire week leading up to this day, and he guessed his buck was holed up in the much thicker scrub that encaged the valley floor on this side. The beast wouldn't be moving much; he would have to find it. This meant plowing into deep thickets where briars and dried-up huckleberry bushes would snag and tear at his clothing, and he would have to silently endure the pain.

Of the countless valleys that defined the intermountain West, this heavily wooded tract in Idaho's panhandle was his favorite, mainly because it was so inaccessible. There were no campgrounds nearby, no fire lookout towers. His trail was an old logging road the Forest Service didn't maintain. Ryan knew very few hunters willing to go to the same lengths for such solitude. That's why it surprised and annoyed him to find fresh human prints along the same ridge he was on. He had climbed the backside of the mountain from the south, while the prints, for as far as he could see them, showed that the other man had hiked a good portion of the ridge from the northeast. Perhaps he had accidentally stumbled upon signs of the big buck; perhaps he had been watching this valley for a long time. Either way, Ryan now had someone else to look out for.

He hunted with the wind in his face, but it was tricky keeping it that way. Sometimes a fallen tree or boulder from a rock slide prevented him from taking the course he wanted, forcing him to cut across it at an angle. Sometimes the wind suddenly changed direction for a moment or longer, gusting from behind or from the side, and when this happened he stood still and waited for it to pass. Each time he then assessed the situation ahead of him, and if it looked okay, and if the wind had resumed its former tack, he slowly proceeded again. If the wind kept its new course, he changed his entirely, tacking back and forth like a sailboat, his eyes on a distant point—a pinnacle of rock or craggy gulch to mark the position he was aiming for. Since wind usually travels uphill, and since deer like to keep it at their faces to smell what's coming, the trick was to get behind them while they moved, so he wanted to gain position on high ground and hunt downhill. A deer's senses of smell and hearing are acute, but Ryan knew if he was careful in his game of windy chess, and also didn't make too much noise, he stood a chance of getting off a decent shot. He just hoped this other hunter wouldn't ruin it for him.

When he had worked his way to a high saddle between two peaks, he set his gun down and allowed himself a moment to drink some water and soak in the view. From where he stood, he could look right down the valley stretching for several miles in a thick green cape that narrowed where the two ridges on either side came together. Beyond, he could see layers of snow-capped mountains stretching like an accordion, each layer growing lighter, mistier, the more distant from him. He could imagine he was standing on the spine of the earth, looking out over the Nepal frontier at some point high in the Himalayas, or over the peaks of the Andes, pictures he had poured over in *National Geographic*. Yet this was his home. These were his mountains. Though he came here often, he never stopped feeling the mystery of the place, the enormity of it. This was as close as he could get to understanding God.

He felt the two-by-four-inch cross hanging on a chain around his neck, between his thermal underwear and wool shirt. His father had fashioned it in his workshop behind their log frame house in the mountains, two thick strips of bronze pounded together and etched by hand with straight horizontal and vertical lines, a severe but clean design. Ryan had yet to tell his father he had been accepted at the state university in Moscow. Though less than a hundred miles away, it was a world apart from their close-knit community, his father's gravel business, his religion—exactly what Ryan wanted. Still, they only had each other. There was so much history between them. Ryan grasped the chain around his neck and wondered if he could break that history by yanking the cross free and tossing it far down the mountain, where, at the bottom, he imagined it working its way through the earth over the eons until it finally reached the earth's boiling metal core and melted, completing the cycle back into nature. He briefly entertained this fantasy before loosening his fingers and letting the cross fall back heavily against his heart. He wasn't ready to face his father.

Ryan had been hunting here for eleven years, ever since his father first brought him along as a pudgy six-year-old with large, awkward hands and feet. His father had seemed so big then, carrying the same rifle Ryan carried now while he had brandished an old pump-style pellet gun. He had fully expected to kill something with it; his father had simply wanted to teach him from a young age the techniques of stalking game, to toughen his legs to the rigors of hiking up steep ravines and through sticky, tangled underbrush, to learn the nuances of gauging wind direction and moving quietly through the forest. Ryan was a good student, soaking up these skills unconsciously the way people learn a foreign language by surrounding themselves with only those who speak it. Soon the language of the mountains and forests became his natural tongue, and he ached to speak it any chance he could, daydreaming his way through school, wishing he were clambering down a summer slope or up a lodgepole pine. The fresh air, exercise, and plentiful wild game were boons to his young body. Now a high school senior, he stood six foot one and weighed 185 pounds, without a trace of baby fat on his hardened frame.

His father was one of the few men who could keep up with him. Daniel McAllister may have stood four inches shorter than his son and weighed thirty pounds less, but he was lean and wiry, like an old coon dog. Slightly bowlegged, he could reach a full sprint in two seconds, and his narrow shoulders carried hunting and camping gear for miles apparently without tiring. He was still larger-than-life to Ryan, who often felt as if he hunted with him even when alone.

Growing up, what Ryan liked best about his father was that he spoke in analogies that were easy to understand. When teaching how to "still hunt," he used the deer as an example.

"Deer stop, look, and listen when they move through the woods," he explained. "So should you."

When they came to faint lines in the forest that indicated a game trail, they followed along, because "if the animals use 'em, so should you."

And by way of explaining the importance of knowing the areas to be hunted and whether they're worth the effort: "You can't hunt what ain't there."

His father hated the idea suggested in many outdoors magazines of using a notepad to record the particulars of an area, instead preferring to commit every detail to memory; he said it forced you to remember the important things that way. He also disdained maps and compasses. He brought them along for emergencies, such as weather that limited visibility, but whenever he could he trained Ryan to orient himself to the sun and features of the terrain—a skill, he said, that had to be developed in case he lost his other tools.

"God gave you the best map and compass up here," he said, tapping his head.

Ryan's earliest memories were of going to a small Catholic church with his parents when he was five years old. He had liked how the pews squeaked in the silence, the priest's earnest arched eyebrows, and though he couldn't always follow what was being read or said, he believed every word. He had especially loved the church's stained glass windows, their panes arranged in basic geometric patterns—no pictures, no symbols, just simple shapes that filtered light in a pleasing way. Ryan liked the pale blue squares best because when the sun lit them from behind, they glowed the color of a mountain sky on a clear day.

It was the one time during the week that the family was together, his right hand in his mother's left, her starched white dress pressed crisply against him and smelling of Downy, his father sitting to his left, the smell of Old Spice, his face full of dark, bristly whiskers he never seemed able to shave off entirely. Though Ryan didn't enjoy the length of the sermons because the straight-backed pews were so hard, he had the advantage of being tall for his age and often entertained himself by sliding low in his seat and touching his feet to the floor, giving him the secret pleasure of feeling grown up.

When his parents began openly fighting, he could hear their yells after he had been put to sleep, starting out muffled at first and then rising in pitch until the anger behind the words could be heard, rising again until individual words sometimes could be made out. His father often swore, some words that Ryan recognized from kids at school and some he'd never heard before, though from their tone he could tell were just as bad.

He would crawl out of bed and tremble at the top of the stairs, listening, afraid of what he might hear, but equally afraid of what he might miss, intent on knowing everything that was going on, as if that gave him some kind of control over the situation. Sometimes he heard crashing sounds, and while he wanted to run downstairs to see what was happening, fear stopped him. He had done that once, and the spanking his father gave him left welts on his bottom that took two days to heal. Instead, he sat at the top of the stairs and prayed as earnestly as he had seen the priest pray every Sunday. He prayed that his parents might stop fighting soon and that the family could be happy again, his eyes shut so tightly because he prayed so hard—not in his head, as he sometimes did, but out loud because he thought it gave his words more power. And the fighting always stopped eventually, the clashing noises subsiding first, the angry voices easing their way into sullen, muffled tones and finally silence, when Ryan could crawl back into bed and fall asleep at last.

But after a while, his prayers began sounding foolish to him, as if he were just talking to himself out loud in the dark. Sometimes he wouldn't pray, just as a test, and he found that the fighting always stopped eventually anyway; so then he began mixing it up, praying during some fights and not during others. The prayers didn't prove to fix things any faster.

Ryan was eight years old when his mother left them. One time when he asked about her, his father didn't say a word, only looked at him as if half listening to someone in the other room. His father never spoke of what happened. He brooded for more than two months, rarely talking to his son and even giving up church. Then after this period he suddenly became light and returned to church regularly, in fact, fervently, with a zeal Ryan had never seen in him before. He started crying out during sermons, "Halleluia!" and "Praise the Lord!"—exaltations that embarrassed Ryan and apparently many other parishioners. They must have asked the priest to do something about it, because Ryan overheard him trying to mention it to his father several times, but his father acted as if he didn't know what the problem was. Abruptly, he began attending a new evangelical church led by a young man with a rosy-cheeked wife and three homely children who offered a whole different style of religion than Ryan was used to. They encouraged emotional displays like his father's and directed a "praise band" that played contemporary rock gospels during services, complete with a drummer and an electric guitarist. His father became a deacon in this new church, one of its most vocal and worshipful parishioners, leading two Bible studies a week, later three.

Outside of church, he became annoyed with things that had never bothered him before, like the condition of Forest Service roads.

"Where does all of our tax money go?" he fumed as they inched along a pothole-filled two-track one day when Ryan was twelve. "We pay for the right to hunt what God gave freely. I'd like to know what those feds are doing with my hard-earned money."

Ryan felt like he should know the answer to his father's question. He looked out the window. All he could see for miles around were mountains and evergreens, and he figured since the name of the agency was the "Forest Service," they must have had something to do with all those pines.

"I think they use the money to plant trees," he offered.

"God plants trees, not the government!" his father roared. "We don't need federal agencies to run a world that was working just fine until we decided to monkey with natural law—"

He cut himself short. He didn't apologize to Ryan but instead reached over and scrubbed the top of his son's head with his knuckles. Ryan kept staring forward with his head bent slightly down.

After they got to their destination and began hiking through the bottom of a slough, the sky darkened. When the first drops of rain fell, Ryan's father only gritted his teeth and didn't say anything, but when the patter became a steady torrent and the ground around them muddy and hard to walk on, he raised his head fiercely to the sky and shook his fist.

"What are you trying to do, drown me?" he yelled.

Ryan quietly slogged along, occasionally glancing at his father's angry face, the uncontrolled way he clenched his fists and bushwhacked through the scrub and tall grasses with noisy fury, ruining any chance of surprising game, if they still had one. Ryan was disgusted at what he saw. He liked the rain, liked the way it brought misty clouds low into the valley, liked the sound of it, the taste. He had come to like cloudy days in general just as much as sunny ones, for the variation of them and because it was another face of nature.

Now, watching the gloom gather over him as a cold front blew in, carrying the foretelling crispness and smell of snow, he wondered if he liked cloudy days because they were vague and bittersweet, like the ache of muscles after a long hike, or the memory of his mother.

In all the time after she left, Ryan could only remember his father talking about her once.

"If it hadn't been for Jesus, son, I don't know how I could have dealt with it. I don't know what…" he said, his voice trailing off.

From the time he was fourteen, Ryan had grown increasingly uncomfortable hunting with his father. Ryan still viewed the wilderness as he always had, with a wide-eyed sense of wonder and awe, but his father had lost that. Where before he had welcomed the coming of winter because it meant he could snowshoe or snowmobile, he now complained before it even snowed, when the first chill winds of autumn brought hints of the season to come. He groaned of the work the cold brought, the chopping of wood, stocking of provisions, and other preparations. He began using maps and compasses on hunting trips and insisted Ryan did, too.

"You just can't foresee certain calamities," he now said.

Two weeks ago he went hunting with Jim Dupree, a long-time member of their church, and both men bagged a buck. Ryan's father had his animal cut into steaks and ground into sausage, but Dupree only mounted the antlers. After the next service, he was confronted by his friend.

"I hear you're wasting some of the bounty the good Lord in His wisdom allowed us to take."

"It weren't wasted, Dan. I got a trophy out of it."

"Why didn't you let me cut it up?"

"You already bagged one of your own, so I didn't figure you needed any."

"Then why not give it to someone else?"

"Where was I going to keep it in the meantime? My freezer's

already full. What's the big deal anyway, Dan? A kill's a kill."

The answer, when it came, was low but insistent.

"If all you want is a trophy, then stick to bowling, Dupree, or entering your squash in the county fair. If I didn't have the love of God in me, I'd put the fear of Him into you right now. I'd beat your ass right now if I didn't love the Lord."

Ryan tensed, waiting for a blow-up. Dupree, a long-haul trucker for a local timber outfit, wasn't a man to back down from a challenge, and his face burned redly. But after staring at his friend for several seconds, he looked away and began mumbling a defense. Ryan's father turned and motioned for his son to follow.

Ryan wanted to be proud of that, for simply walking away, but at the same time was confused, even frightened, by the way his father had looked at Dupree: without anger, not even pity, but with a burning blankness in his dark eyes. He had looked at the man as if he didn't exist. Just like Ryan's mother. Ryan felt lightheaded with the superstitious thought that maybe his father had a direct link to God, that maybe he held the power to condemn people to hell by simply forgetting them and thus wiping them from God's memory in the process. It was illogical, even ridiculous, yet Ryan couldn't help wondering what would happen when he left.

A flash of movement on the slope below caught his eye, and he looked down at the largest buck he had ever seen, even in pictures, with an antler rack that seemed to carry the spires of a dozen cathedrals. The buck was moving along the edge of the forest, munching on the vegetation that grew where light could penetrate, apparently unaware of Ryan, who felt a flush of anger for setting his rifle down. He bent low and duck-walked to where it lay against a boulder, checking to make sure it was loaded. Then with it held before him he crawled on his belly back up the incline and peeked over the edge of the ridge.

The huge shadow that had loomed there had vanished.

He scanned the location. There were only two places the buck could have gone: down a narrow ravine that snaked behind a line of aspen or into the forest. To get to either required crossing rocky open ground and chance being seen and heard. But the sky had mostly grayed, the air grown colder, and with the wind now blowing hard in Ryan's face, the buck certainly wasn't going to turn around and come up the slope, so Ryan as quickly and silently as he could scampered over the ridge and down the mountain.

To his left stood a sheer granite cliff about fifty feet high, to his right a much higher cliff holding up a bowl packed with snow all the way to the edge of an overhanging shelf about twenty feet wide. The slope he negotiated was covered with a smooth crust of snow spiked with talus colored the same iron-red as the right-hand cliff; rocky stubble occasionally clattered under his boots despite his best efforts to walk quietly, but he just gritted his teeth and kept moving. This buck was too awesome to lose; he was surprised to have seen him at all. The wind was now blowing hard, and flurries of snow trickled onto his neck, forcing him to pull his collar more tightly around him. Once he got to the edge of the woods, he walked to the spot where he had last seen the deer and then a little further, looking for signs that would show him the way. He then worked his way back in the other direction, his eyes intent on the ground, the low-lying bushes, and the trunks of the trees, all at once when possible, in sweeping glances. His patience was rewarded when he found a juniper bush with its dark berries and branches freshly stripped. There Ryan plunged into the forest.

As soon as he passed the wall of trees, the wind instantly melted, replaced with a silence that stopped him. As his ears adjusted, the tiniest pattering sounds became distinct, of snow falling softly upon pine boughs or to the ground, the creaking of the high trees and swishing of the wind in their uppermost branches. He moved into the forest slowly, scanning the ground for deer sign, occasionally stopping and looking about him into the murk ahead. The day had become dark, and thick clouds gray with snow swooped in over the valley. Though his hands were cold, he only pulled his skin-tight shooting gloves from his pockets, saving the warmer but bulkier wool mittens for after his hoped-for kill.

To stalk game this way was slow going, and Ryan moved like a blind man groping through the twists and turns of a stranger's house. Though this valley was familiar to him, there was no way he could cover every square inch of it even if he spent the rest of his life trying; there would always be an uncharted gully or ravine, a surprising rise in terrain, a different fallen log, a fresh slide where snow in winter or mud in spring had ripped another path—always a new angle to take even on familiar ground. As it was, he had entered a part of the forest unknown to him.

At one point, he found a game trail, and from the indication of droppings nearby, it was used by deer. Generally, Ryan would have followed it, but he knew big bucks like his usually avoided the more common trails. Instead, he tried to think like an old deer, staring intently into the thickest brush for a sign of where it would have gone. And he was slow enough and patient enough to find it: a freshly broken branch here, newly turned soil there, prints in the soft earth that led him ever deeper into the thicket. The wind had almost stopped entirely, and while he continued to monitor it, he wasn't sure if this would do any good. He was sweating heavily now, and his scent would carry far. Luck was going to have to be with him.

Ryan stalked for over an hour. As he constantly had to stop to measure what there was of the wind or take bearings on his compass, he guessed he had only moved a quarter of a mile or so into the forest, though he couldn't see the edge of it when he looked behind him. He turned his head back around at a noise in front of him. Something was scratching in a pile of leaves not more than twenty yards ahead—rustling and pausing, rustling and pausing. Ryan brought his rifle level to his waist. He stood completely still, only his breath moving, forming intermittent clouds before evaporating into wispy vines. He stood still for so long he could feel himself weaving on his own feet, an involuntary, nearly imperceptible swaying that felt more exaggerated to him because he was trying so hard to contain it. For just one brief moment his right heel rocked back and snapped a brittle twig in half—and suddenly there was an explosion of leaves and a cacophony of squawking, and he swung his rifle in front of him in self-defense, the racket sounded as if it were moving right over him! Then he caught the smell of wet feathers, and two of them, both gray flecked with black and white, floated by his face, and he realized he had spooked a wild turkey as it rooted only feet away. The damp earth had muffled the sound, making it seem it came from farther off.

That's when he saw the buck about fifty yards upwind, nose and ears twitching, in brush at the bottom of the small rise Ryan stood on. He saw the whole of it only in pieces as it moved, carrying a set of antlers that held at least sixteen points, the two main horns sprouting from the skull like horny clubs. It was the size of a small horse, chestnut red in color, with a sheening coat and powerful haunches that looked as though they could launch it over gorges twenty feet wide, and probably had. Two wide scars ran down its flank, signs of monumental battles fought, and won. Its face looked judicial, softened somewhat by a grandfatherly quality, with gray splashed about the muzzle.

Ryan saw all this from behind the sights and down the end of his rifle barrel. The buck stood in silhouette at a slight angle. His father's words flashed through his mind, not as words but as a conditioned feeling:

"You're not aiming just to shoot a deer but to kill it. If you don't have your sights on a vital, don't even think about pulling the trigger. I won't have you wasting good meat out here with a poor shot. God abhors waste, son."

Though Ryan didn't have a clear shot, he felt he might not ever get a better chance at a buck this size. He held it in his sights for a full five seconds, his finger stayed lightly on the trigger. His mind couldn't help straying ahead to the problem of how he was going to get this beast out of the forest; even field dressed, it would still form a much larger package than he could carry. He became aware that his heart was pounding and his finger involuntarily tugging at the trigger. He knew he could hit this great hulking shadow, he just wasn't sure he could kill it. The buck took a hesitant step forward, exposing his heart through a break in the snow-covered bushes. Ryan took a slow, shuddering breath, moved his rifle a fraction of an inch—the buck bolted in the opposite direction and was instantly gone.

The hunt was over. Ryan didn't bother to check the wind or walk quietly as he tracked his way back through the forest to where he had entered it. The rest of the day, the few hours left before dusk, would be spent as a pleasant hike. What had alerted the buck—a whiff of Ryan's nervous sweat, the slightest dull reflection off his gun barrel? It didn't matter. He knew this was something he could never talk about, that he had just enjoyed his own private story. No one would believe it. He realized such an animal is a myth until it's killed; only then does it become living, in the sense of being real. In some ways, he was almost unsure he had even seen it.

He was in a reverie when he reentered the talus field at the base of the rust-colored cliff. Still several hundred yards away from the ridge he was aiming for, he heard the crack of a rifle behind him, surprising him, but only momentarily, for the shot echoed from the cliff and in a second was followed by another loud crack. A slab of ice and snow shot from the bowl like a wall of water through a broken dike. Ryan knew he couldn't outrun the avalanche, that he should try to stay on top of it by using swimming motions, but he couldn't help turning to run anyway. He saw the buck leap from the forest straight toward him and then suddenly veer, hesitate, and swerve back. The racing white wave rumbled, and the ground shook, and the gun flew from his hands as he was hit and began swimming, furiously kicking, gasping for air, chunks of snow and dirt and ice in his nose and mouth, his body pelted and stabbed by small pebbles and larger rocks, the world a whirl about him as he tumbled down the mountain.

Just as suddenly he found himself in absolute stillness. Dazed, he tried to sit up, but his head hit something jagged, and he panicked when he realized he couldn't see a thing and had no idea which end was up. He struggled wildly, irrationally, adrenaline shrieking through his body, but when he lodged his right hand between his hip and an ice-cold wall, he froze, panting heavily, his pulse pounding in his neck, his stomach clenched in the absolute terror of the moment.

Even in the face of this terror, he knew he had to calm down, to spare whatever oxygen he had. With great effort he forced himself to stop gulping air. Next, he concentrated on slowing his shallow breathing even more until after some minutes it had settled into a still rapid but more rhythmic pace. Only then did his training fully take over, and he began assessing his situation. That he could breathe at all told him he was either buried shallowly or trapped in a small cavity, otherwise the pressure of the snow would have crushed him already or slowly be squeezing his chest, suffocating him. His torso rested in a space just large enough for him to twist partly in either direction and with effort bring his right hand to his chest, but his legs and left arm were pinned tightly enough to prevent him from doing more than move them slightly from side to side. He then began to feel the pains in his body, as if he were naked and scraped raw, his skin stripped away, leaving only the hard edges of bone and excruciatingly soft nerve endings exposed. He soon realized he was still clothed and that his pain was caused by the small movements of fabric over skin. His head felt like a balloon, unnaturally large upon his body, separate from it even, tied only by the string of his neck where all his blood seemed to be pumping. It ached so much, the throbbing was almost sweet. The only place he didn't feel any pain was in his right leg, which was numb from mid-thigh down.

With his right hand, he felt for the hunting knife that had been strapped to his side. It was gone, and while difficult to tell, it didn't feel as if his digital watch remained around his left wrist, either. As well as he could, he groped around his tight space for his backpack or any of the equipment it had contained, his compass, water bottle, box of cartridges, keys—anything he could dig with—but evidently it had all been carried away by the avalanche.

He lay there for a moment, struggling to keep his breathing slow and think. He had to conserve his energy—if his core body temperature went down, he was doomed—but he also couldn't wait for help. The hunter who had triggered the avalanche probably hadn't seen him, for if he had, he wouldn't have shot in that direction. By the time his father missed him and sent a crew to locate him, it could take days before they found the exact spot where he lay buried. There was no way around it; he would have to claw his way out. To orient himself, he spit. Because he was already wet and effectively blind, it took him several tries before he was able to determine which way was up. The chamber's roof pressed at the back of his skull, and, jackknifed at the waist, he had to twist awkwardly to scratch at the icy surface. Soon his fingers went numb, and his fingernails cracked and broke. It was like clawing at sandstone. Shavings of ice rained upon him as he worked, but after what seemed half an hour, though it might have been only five minutes, he knew it was useless. He had barely scraped out a hollow large enough to lay his hand in flat. He stopped and tried to subdue another panic attack before letting loose in a frenzy, heaving his body up and down as if he could shake his would-be tomb off its icy foundations, watch the walls crumble all around him. He pounded his fist against the roof until his hand grew warm and he tasted spatters of blood, and he screamed so loudly he hurt his own ears and left them ringing even after he stopped.

All of his thrashing loosened the necklace that had been thrown back behind his head from the force of his fall, and now he felt the heavy homemade cross cold through his T-shirt. Quickly, he unwrapped the chain from around his neck and, being careful not to drop it, grasped it in his right hand and used it to chip at the ice, gripping the lower, longer half at the crosspiece, wielding it like a knife. The cold metal warmed slightly in his grip, and flecks of ice fell about his body.

He made some headway with this new method but soon ran into another problem: how to dispose of his diggings. Small piles of ice packed tightly around him, making it even more difficult to work. He knew he couldn't eat this; as thirsty as he was, it would chill his insides and dangerously lower his body temperature. He was going to have to inch his way upward in a slow but steady routine of chipping, piling the ice and snow into the corners, jamming chunks of dirt and rocks and twigs into the frozen walls around him as he moved into the space opening above him.

Eventually, he carved out enough room so that he could sit up. Now that his torso was free, he began chopping at the material around his waist and legs. He brought his arm forward and back, forward and back, stopping only long enough to occasionally switch hands until, after so much dogged work, the cross broke at the tip. He didn't even know this until he accidentally stabbed himself in the thigh with what was now effectively a razor-sharp dagger, but he was covered with so many wounds he hardly felt this one. To his relief, the work went a little more quickly with his newly shaped tool.

How long had it been since he'd left his home in search of the massive buck, since he'd been buried underneath the pile of ice and snow and part of the mountain? Time had become absolutely, nonsensically irrelevant. The darkness remained absolute around him, and he had no idea if it was because he was buried so hopelessly deep or because night had fallen outside. Maybe he was only inches away from breaking through and didn't know it because there was no light to shine through the wall of ice. That's what he told himself to keep working. His own voice in the darkness was comforting.

However long he had been buried, there had been enough air for him so far, and he guessed there was a hidden vent feeding his chamber, so he stopped in his work of digging to briefly explore it. It was now large enough to turn around in, and he found it was much more irregularly shaped than he had first supposed, with many nooks and crannies running off from the tiny main cell. He thought he felt a boulder behind him to his left, and, just barely through a small fissure above that, the woody husk of a pine tree—whether fallen or standing, he couldn't tell. These obstacles must have provided enough of a break to keep him from being totally buried, and if there were a series of fissures leading to air, they might also lead him to freedom. Whether this was true or his wishful thinking, he was still alive, though ravenously hungry. He worked until so fatigued he could no longer raise his arm above him.

The panic attacks seemed to be over. Though he wasn't any more comfortable or sure of his escape, such feelings didn't matter. He simply did what he had to in order to survive, and his terror subsided. In some ways, he felt a calm he had never felt before, and he wondered if this wasn't what dying was all about. The thought of death no longer scared him. He was a mole now, an icy mole. Home, the smell of freshly cut tamarack, the fireplace's warm glow, daylight, moonlight—all were memories from a past life long ago, long before he came to his new home in the ice.

When he awoke—an hour or a day later—it seemed as if the

blackness was a little more gray than it had been before he drifted off. At first, he was ecstatic, and then despondent. What if his eyes were just playing tricks on him? Immediately the air around him seemed as black as night, and his spirits fell, but a few moments later, after he had stopped digging to wipe his brow, it seemed lighter again—not enough to actually see anything, but the blackness wasn't as oppressive. He tried to find the source of this perceived light, lightness really, but couldn't, and he decided to forget about it and go back to chipping. As he continued to work, he became certain it was actually as black as before—maybe even blacker—and he kept thinking like this until he felt the sun, like everything he could remember, had disappeared, carried away by the leading edge of the avalanche, and it was only by some miracle or curse that he hadn't been swept over the edge of the world with everything else. And despair overcame him again, and he began crying softly in the blackness, uncontrollably. Then he stopped, giving in to the notion that he was dead, but he resurrected and with a fervor began picking again at the ice, still crying for everything he had lost and for what he had been, crying for what he was now, miserable and hungry and cold, crying because he couldn't help it, it was natural, and as the tears trickled down his face, he blasted at the wall he knew was in front of him though he couldn't see it, and he felt the broken cross dig into the ice as if into flesh, flecks of it falling away, and then chunks, and he threw himself into the act of digging like a man no longer in control, and he was both of those now—no longer in control and a man—and his arm continued moving forward on its own even after his eyes fell shut, his hands moving forward even after his arms fell to his side, and he slowly, unconsciously crawled up into the tunnel he had carved and collapsed.

He dreamed of a faraway place called Idaho, seeing the bristly gray face of a man appear before him—his father?—listening to voices speak to him louder and louder until finally they woke him and he was again in blackness and terror before he banged his head and with a crack of intense light blasted himself back into his restless dreams. The name Dan popped up, and he thought he might be Dan; then he was sure of it; then he saw the body of a magnificent deer and knew he wasn't Dan but was Deer, and he said it out loud, "Deer," repeating it until he saw the word "Dear" in front of him, and he thought *dear God dear God* until he knew God was gone and he was in hell, that's why these cold demons tore at him, he never even wondered that it wasn't the hellfire his father had warned him of. Then he realized Daniel was his father and the deer a part of them both that, in all the time since original sin, had never left them, and original sin was nothing more than forgetfulness of that, a forgetting followed by a deep sleep.

He saw a field of pale blue before him, and at first he wasn't sure he was awake, but he shook his head and felt the icy ache of it, his cheeks red-raw and numb, tiny stalactites in his hair breaking up as he moved, and he knew he was awake. He opened his eyes completely, the wall in front of him glowing a translucent blue from the sunlight sheening behind it. Before collapsing he must have tunneled his way to within inches of freedom. Refreshed now with the certainty of his release, he chipped until the wall crumbled, and then he punched a hole big enough to squirm out of, wiggling like a moth from a cocoon.

Above him, the sky was a cloudless icy blue, full of sun, and the trees around him sparkled with reflected light. The whole slide area glistened in this new snow, and he wanted to whoop for joy, but his throat was so sore and he so weak, he could only choke a whisper before setting off a jag of coughing.

When he finally stopped he saw the buck standing directly in front of him only a few yards away.

The great beast didn't run, hardly moved at all except to expel a thunderhead of steam from its nostrils. It stood knee-deep in the snow, its massive coat crusted with icicles and frost, which also hung from its muzzle—a crystalline statue. Ryan couldn't tell if the buck had also been caught in the avalanche, though it appeared just as weak as if it, too, had suffered and struggled and now could do nothing more than stand and watch this other. But deep in its eyes moved an alertness and shimmering, a greater life than Ryan had ever seen.

She Was a Winter

It had come as a complete surprise to Elly when her mother said, "I don't know if it makes sense to stick me in the ground, dear. I think I'd be better off mixed into my annual flower garden. Or even," and here she giggled, "scattered to the *four winds*." With those last words, she opened her eyes wide and threw her arms apart as if to hug her daughter. Elly instinctively leaned back in her chair. It wasn't like her mother to be so touchy feely, to giggle even, though she otherwise seemed lucid.

That had been last month, the cancer seemingly in remission, over coffee in the small but bright and airy kitchen of the 1920s brownstone Elly had grown up in. She had later thought once or twice about asking her mother if she should write that idea into her will, but something had always come up. Then death came, and it was too late.

Elly stood now in a large room filled with a wordless synthesized melody and a soft glow from the recessed lighting along the top length of the walls. Her mother lay in a polished mahogany casket on a large dais nearly invisible under bouquets of roses, irises, lilies. A long row of mourners filed past, lingering, and Elly could hear their low but firm enthusiasms on how *good* her mother looked. It was two thirty. In half an hour they would drive the casket to the cemetery where her father was buried so that they could be interred side by side. Afterward everyone would enjoy a catered buffet.

Something didn't feel right to Elly, though she was unable to pinpoint exactly what. The funeral home staff seemed more than competent; they were serious but pleasant and very attentive. They had taken care of all the arrangements, the drinks, the appetizers, even a wheelchair for Aunt Marion with a smartly dressed teenaged boy to push her around. Everything appeared perfect.

Everything was too perfect. Elly walked over to the casket and looked at her mother's body apparently so comfortably reclined, dressed in arguably her best outfit, a smart navy pantsuit, though that had been a gift and one she had rarely worn in life. Elly had tried to tell the mortician that, but perhaps she hadn't made herself clear. Most strange was her mother's face, her closed eyelids generously swathed in an eye shadow that matched the pantsuit, her lips a dark wine red. Elly sensed what the mortician had done; he had recognized that her mother possessed a winter complexion, not a summer one as she had always fancied herself to have, and now rightly made up she did look more beautiful than Elly could remember. Only she didn't look like herself. For the last fifteen years, her mother had worn the same powder blue Mary Kay eye shadow and pale pink Mary Kay lipstick she had regularly bought from Aunt Adelia.

That's when it occurred to Elly that the flowers were perennials, every one. They were traditional and beautiful, but where were the marigolds and sunflowers her mother had loved so much, had so carefully cultivated in the sandy glacial till in her backyard? There wasn't even one arrangement of zinnias. And the music—what instrument was it that made such a noise, so soothing it had become grating? Where was the Boston Pops her mother had never tired of? Arthur Fiedler or John Williams, it wouldn't have mattered. She was sure she had made that clear to the mortician.

He walked up to her now, lightly gesturing toward the body before reclasping his hands. "She was a beautiful woman, especially for her age," he said.

It had been a long time since Elly had smoked a cigarette, but she suddenly craved one. "Yes," she agreed. "It's just—it's just that she didn't normally wear—she didn't normally choose such—"

"Ah," the mortician said, his left hand on his right elbow, his right index finger pressed to his nose. He was pursing his lips, but to Elly, it looked as if he were suppressing a smile. "She was clearly a winter. I simply took the liberty of enhancing what nature had so generously given her."

He had been a makeup artist in several local theaters, even the Cleveland Opera for a time, and was regarded as the best mortician in the city. He and his staff had done, were still doing, a wonderful job. What was she complaining about?

She felt a deep heaviness, a heaviness she hadn't felt in years. Is this what it means to grieve? she wondered. She smoothed her dress over her tall, trim figure. People had always told her she looked like her mother, and she had never understood this; they had never been able to see the true nature of her mother's coloring. Elly had always been a summer, a real summer, even with her red hair, which still seemed new to her though she had dyed it way back when she got her divorce. She liked her cute bob, how it curled around her face and framed it. Her mother had hated it.

Yes, she was a winter, but she had thought she was a summer, and now the summer was gone. Elly looked at the body again, and it seemed almost comical to her. It was a prop in a play, a wax dummy in a museum. Who would call a lump of wool or wax Mother? Where had her mother gone?

She couldn't help thinking of the line from Luke: "Let the dead bury their dead." It had always puzzled her, and now seeing her pastor in a rare moment alone, she approached him and asked about it. But as soon as the question was out, she found herself going on about something else that had caught her fancy years ago as an exchange student in France. She had lived in a region known as Cathar country, after the thirteenth-century Christian Gnostics. The Cathars didn't believe in selling earth for the burial of the dead, which they equated with such practices as selling pardons for one's sins. For these beliefs, among many others, they were hunted down by the Inquisition. Some were burned alive. But they accepted this fate readily, without reservations, because they believed their souls were then freed from their bodies. Isn't that what Jesus taught? she asked her pastor. That it's the inner, not the outer, that counts?

After listening patiently, he politely but firmly made it clear there was a reason those people were called heretics, and that God alone, not belief in a heretical sect, can free us from our bodies. He then went on to explain, quite eruditely, how the mind can easily conjure up fantastical explanations during times of emotional stress—especially when the stress is caused by suppressing emotions. He never even got to Luke. Elly made a mental note never to mention the Cathars to her pastor again.

At that moment cousin Margaret walked up and put a hand on her shoulder.

"How are you doing? Okay?"

Let the dead bury their dead, she was thinking. "Hm?"

"I know, this is hard for all of us."

"Do you think maybe I should have had Mother cremated?"

Margaret took a step back. "My God! What made you think of that?"

"It's something she asked for herself," Elly said quickly.

"That doesn't sound like Aunt Cecy."

"We were having coffee one morning. It was toward the end."

"She was *sick*, Elly." Margaret shuddered. "It just seems like something pagans would do, you know, like cannibals roasting you for dinner. My god, can we talk about something else?"

Cremated. It was an awful-sounding word, Elly agreed. As if they turned you into a paste. They both lapsed into silence.

"She looks so beautiful," Margaret said at last, reverently, "just like a movie star, the older one in that movie, you know which one I'm talking about?"

Elly repressed a sigh. This fixation on the body, body, body. It was driving her crazy. She remembered when she was a teenager and for some months had actually forced herself to throw up after meals. Neither of her parents seemed to notice for a long time, but one day, when Elly was beginning to feel tired and dizzy at school, her mother said, "I don't know what you're doing, sweetheart, but you look so *good*. You're not fat anymore."

She felt very heavy now as if the ceiling were pressing down upon her shoulders, squeezing the air out of the room.

"Hi, kiddo."

She recognized the crisp, high-pitched voice of Uncle Drake and turned to kiss him on the cheek. She was running out of things to say to all these people, but as Margaret had wandered off in search of a restroom, Elly ventured to bring up her mother's wish again.

"Cecilia would never have said *that*," Uncle Drake said with his insurance salesman's assurance. "She'll be happy buried next to Dick, I guarantee it. When your Aunt Adelia and I go, that's what we want."

"But you'll be dead," Elly said, now beginning to feel exasperated. "What will you care where your body is?"

"It isn't polite to talk about dead people at a funeral, you know," he nearly whispered.

"My mother can't hear us," Elly said loudly, feeling a little dizzy with her boldness. She motioned toward the casket. "It's just a body."

Uncle Drake stared at her as if she had thrown cold water in his face. "It's your mother!" he exclaimed. Then his look softened, and a sad smile played across his lips. "You're grieving, I know. This is a difficult time for all of us." His eyes quickly flicked to the side and then returned. "Excuse me, your Aunt Adelia is calling for me."

Did anyone here really know her mother? Elly wondered. Did they know of the constant little side comments, about Elly's figure, her hair, the way she drove, her choice of boyfriends? There had been a terrific battle just to be able to go to France. Later, when she had finally developed the courage to divorce her first husband, her mother scolded her for not trying hard enough and then called him behind Elly's back to arrange a reconciliation.

When she found a man she actually trusted and loved, the first question her mother asked was, "What does he do for a living?"

"He's a freelance writer," Elly replied.

"Well," her mother chirped. "You'll certainly lose some weight now."

Did they know all that? That though her mother and father would soon lie side by side for eternity, for the last twelve years of their lives together they slept in separate beds? All of this, yet she did have one of the readiest and prettiest smiles. In those rare times when the camera captured a truly spontaneous and exuberant moment, Elly could see that smile on her own lips.

A figure, she didn't bother to turn and see who, stood beside her. A hand gestured.

"Look at her. She really looks good, don't you think?"

"That's not her!" Elly almost shouted.

It was her husband, George.

"Are you okay?" he asked.

The flow of soothing-grating music continued, the smell of

perennials hung uninterrupted in the air, but the room became noticeably quieter, less active, at least to Elly. The mortician turned briefly from his task of directing an assistant, and her pastor, standing nearby, offered a searing look of Christian concern. Margaret dropped something. Uncle Drake paused in mid-sentence while Aunt Adelia patted her curly beehive. At the far end of the room, though in the center of it all, was her mother.

He was right, Elly suddenly thought.

"Jesus was right," she found herself saying out loud. Her pastor caught some of this and smiled.

"Yes," he said, "Jesus is right beside your mother."

Elly hardly heard him. They can do what they like, she was thinking. Six feet under or upon the four winds—it didn't matter. In her own way, she had become just as obsessed with makeup and pantsuits and flowers as they had. Later, she tried to picture her mother, her strict figure softening as it bent over her annual garden, her gloved hands plunging into the earth, but that was not the place for her. Nothing could ever grow there. It looked as if it were going to rain. Elly squinted into the clouds, leaned against her husband, and pulled her collar up against the cold November wind. Then she dropped the first handful of dirt on the coffin.

Making Love While Levitating
Three Feet in the Air

It was Greg's idea to jump out of an airplane and have sex while falling to the ground at 110 miles per hour. Minnie wanted nothing to do with it.

"Are you sure that's even legal?" she asked between bites of her chicken Caesar sandwich, which Greg squinted at before responding. Right away she felt defensive. It was *that* squint, the one where his dark eyebrows twitched over his blue eyes, that indicated he was thinking of something totally unrelated to what they were talking about.

"Of course," he said. "Maybe. It has to be. You can do practically anything you want nowadays. You know, in some countries they have live sex acts right on stage in public. A buddy of mine who went to Thailand when he was in the Navy says—"

"And another thing," Minnie interrupted, glancing over the partition by her left elbow and at the older couple lunching silently in the next booth. The man's shiny pink head, a tiny seashell of a hearing aid in his right ear, was inclined toward her, and though the restaurant was otherwise full of chatter and clattering dishes, she lowered her voice. "You know I hate the term 'having sex.' Sex isn't something you *have*. You can't keep it when it's done. Can't you say, 'making love' instead? It's more accurate, let alone sounds better."

"Sure," Greg said, squinting again, "but we're getting off the subject." He sipped his black coffee and shook his head as if amazed. "Man, that would be something."

As she took another bite of her sandwich, she remembered a scene from a video of real-life accidents—she hadn't wanted to see it, it was on at a party thrown by one of her ex-husband Leroy's friends—where a man whose parachute didn't open hit the ground so hard he bounced. She wasn't convinced Greg was serious about his proposition, but in the same unexplained way she'd kept her eyes on the TV, she couldn't resist asking another question. "How fast did you say we'd fall?"

"One hundred and ten miles per hour. That's terminal velocity, while in an arched position, anyway. It would be a little slower at first; it takes a few seconds to get cranking, although if we shot down head first it would be faster—more streamlined, less resistance."

"Where do you get this kind of information?"

"A pilot friend of mine does this all the time. I'm sure he'd take us up, no questions asked."

"Absolutely not."

"We would jump tandem."

She certainly wasn't going to have his pilot friend and whoever else was up there, and whoever else was down here, see her naked in some harness. Not that she had anything to hide, she assured herself. She sunbathed during the summer—in her bikini, no less, not the one-piece. That she did so in between the house and the fence where no one could see her, and only for the twenty minutes or so the sun actually peeked into that corner of the yard, was because it wouldn't do to have her neighbors gawking at her. Who would buy insurance from a plaything? As to the twenty minutes, any more would probably be bad for her anyway. She had a pretty good body, she felt, a very good body for a thirty-two-year-old. Although her legs were a little short, they were strong. She made sure of that, running three nights a week and working out at the gym another two. Not many women with a kid had legs like hers; she wouldn't let them go slack. And their sex was good, too—their love-making. Greg was complimentary, said all the right things, made her feel special. She felt no desire to crank up the excitement. But she did want him to seem more enthusiastic about Bryan.

"No," she said.

"I see," he said, nodding his head. "Just like that Alaska trip we never took." He leaned forward and flicked a hand at her sandwich. "When are you going to order something different here? I don't think I've seen you get anything else."

"I didn't realize that," she said stiffly, setting the sandwich on her plate and wiping both hands on the napkin over her lap. "I'm glad you pay attention to what I eat. At least you pay attention to that."

He looked at her unblinkingly, his eyebrows twitching, and then barked out a laugh.

"I was kidding, about the parachute thing," he said without smiling. "I just wanted to see if you would do it."

What has gotten into him lately? Minnie wondered as she drove through noontime traffic and back to work in her Chrysler K car—Jenny, she'd named it, maroon, a redhead just like her. She'd bought it before her divorce, before she'd built up a successful business, and while she could afford a better car now, she couldn't let go of Jenny. It wasn't her ideal—that would be a maroon

Ford Taurus—but it was so dependable. Greg was beginning to become the opposite, his ideas wilder and more impractical, as if he were goading her on with them for some reason. When she first met him at a Rotary Club charity auction six months ago, she was convinced she'd discovered the man of her dreams. Barrel-chested, broad-shouldered, and with short, curly hair, he was handsome, but she found his enthusiasm over a handmade quilt most attractive. They made love less than a month later, by far the soonest she'd ever done something like that. She even had an orgasm with him the first time out. It was because they had actually talked: he seemed to know so many interesting people and be up on so many different things. This naturally went with being a paramedic—emergency medical technician; she always forgot to call it that. Afterward, as they lay spooned together in bed, his right arm draped over her body, his hand curled gently around her breast, she asked him what his previous day had been like.

He took a deep breath, and she could feel him looking past her shoulder. Then he dropped his head and began speaking in a low voice, drawing his right index finger over the cotton sheets. Unlike the others, the knuckle on this finger was flattened and jutted from the side in a rounded triangular point toward the middle finger.

"A guy ran a red light and smashed into a woman and her baby. The baby was in a car seat, thank God, or else he would have gone through the window. Happens all the time, right? But the poor little guy was pinned inside. Six months old, he was screaming his tiny lungs out. It took a while, but the other guys and I pulled him free. There was a lot of blood. The bastard who ran the red light didn't have a scratch. He was drunk."

She rolled over to face him, her hand flattening the thick nest of hair on his chest.

"My God! Is the baby all right?"

"He's fine. So's his mother. They're both in the hospital and doing fine."

"You're a hero," she said, surprised at the awe she felt.

She kissed him on the lips, two unmoving bumps of flesh, before turning back around and snuggling into his body, pulling his arm to where it had been. She couldn't help staring at his hand: large, with canned-sausage fingers and protruding knuckles—except for the one on his index finger—and yet incredibly soft. His nails weren't chewed off but trimmed, not too short, either. She liked that. He wasn't too compulsive, she thought. And there it was, that hand she could almost smell a baby's living scent on, cradling her breast so lightly she couldn't even feel his calluses.

The problems hadn't started until the beginning of summer. That's when he brought up the idea of driving the entire way from Spokane to Alaska's Denali National Park and Mount McKinley.

"It's the highest point in North America," he said, the first time she'd heard his resonant voice crack.

"What are we going to drive? Not Jenny, that's for sure."

"My pickup."

"Your pickup," she repeated flatly.

"It's a four-wheel drive. It'll make it. We'll only be gone for two weeks."

"Two weeks? We'd spend most of it on the road."

"This is kind of thing you do for the *experience*, to get out of town for awhile. When was the last time you even took a day off work?"

This caught her off guard. Thinking quickly, she couldn't remember, but what did he expect, putting her on the spot like that? She had certainly taken at least one day off since they'd been together.

"We met just before Christmas," Greg said, "and I remember thinking it was strange you only took Christmas Eve and Christmas Day off, and at the time you told me you'd done the same thing the year before. So it's been what, at least two years?"

"Maybe," she said, but she thought angrily, *You don't get it.* Work wasn't a burden, it was freeing; it had purchased her freedom from a bad marriage. After six months she had known it wouldn't work with Leroy, but it took her seven years to divorce him— seven years of business school, earning her insurance license, and establishing a client base, all while raising Bryan. She had too many responsibilities—her son, herself, her company, her clients; she couldn't allow herself to grow slack. So she hadn't taken a vacation in two years. That was the price she paid to remain beholden to no one, to no man. She was attracted to Greg because she wanted to be; it wasn't like gravity. There was just too much to do at the office. And didn't he realize there were practical considerations where a twelve-year-old was involved?

"What about Bryan?" she asked.

Now Greg seemed taken aback. After a moment he said, "Bring him along."

"No, I can't," she said emphatically. "The three of us in your pickup? Anyway, two weeks is too long. Maybe we can go to Nelson instead?"

"Great. Trade my fortnight for a weekend. What's wrong with Alaska? We'd have a great time. Bryan would have a great time."

"Bryan does not make those kinds of decisions."

Looking back on it now as she drove, she realized she hadn't meant for it to sound that way, so cold. Their relationship had cooled considerably since then; they hadn't made love for more than two weeks. She planned on remedying that tonight.

Minnie sat on her sofa with Greg's head in her lap, stroking his hair. "I was thinking," she said, "that maybe you'd like to stay for dinner. I've got fixings for spaghetti, a bottle of white zinfandel, and something special for dessert. What do you say?"

"Depends on what's for dessert," Greg said without opening his eyes.

"Well, I know you like chocolate," she murmured, playfully drawing a finger over his chest. "And strawberries."

He sat up and made a groaning noise. "And you were thinking of serving it—how?" When she told him, he drew her face near and kissed her, sucking on her lower lip.

"Skip the dinner," he said.

Minnie smiled. She liked it when he played along with her.

"Bryan will be pleased to hear you're staying."

"Yeah, Bryan's a great kid." Greg moved onto the next cushion and reached for the sports page on the coffee table. "I feel kind of stupid asking you this," he said, rustling the paper loudly as he folded it back, "but I want to make sure I'm clear on what's going on tonight. You just want me to stay for dinner, right?"

"Well, yes," she said slowly. "But I don't know why you're saying 'just.'"

"I'm just making sure I know what you're expecting of me."

"Expecting? I'm inviting you to stay for dinner. There aren't any strings attached."

"Dinner, and nothing more."

"I damn well hope there's something more!" She listened carefully for the sounds of Bryan playing Nintendo in the downstairs family room and then continued in a slightly lower tone of voice, "Greg, what is going on with you?"

"It's been awhile since we've, you know, *made love*." He spoke the last two words in an exaggerated, dopey voice, without lifting his eyes from the sports page, and Minnie wasn't sure why he seemed embarrassed to say it.

"Is there some reason we can't make love tonight?"

"Hey, like I said, Bryan's a great kid."

"What's Bryan got to do with this?"

Greg finally put the paper down, but he still spoke to the spaces around Minnie. "When he was in school things were different, but now that summer's here, we've always done it at my place. So I just assumed—"

"Assumed what?" Minnie was so angry she forgot to lower her voice. "You know, there are thousands—no, millions, maybe even *billions* of couples all over the world who have children and also have sex. In fact, one phenomenon actually produces the other."

Greg leaned back on the couch. "I thought sex wasn't something you could have."

"Leroy and I *had sex* all the time," she lied. "It wasn't great, but we still had it."

"Pretty low, Minnie, bringing up another man like that."

"I don't know what else to do." She was suddenly on the verge of crying. "You're scaring me. I thought you wanted a long-term relationship, but if we're going to stay together, you have to feel comfortable around my son. We're a package. You and I might as well forget it if the mere mention of his name—"

"I like Bryan," Greg put in quickly. "I just don't feel right having sex—making love—*messing around* when he's around."

Minnie ran her fingers in the chasm between the cushions they each sat on. "And why not?" *Because you're scared, too,* she thought. Why couldn't he just say it? Leroy had never been able to admit anything like that either, but she'd had such high hopes that Greg was different, especially after how well they had communicated with each other early in their relationship.

"Well," he said after a long pause, "my job can be hard sometimes, real hard."

"What?" She jammed both hands between the cushions and kept them there.

"It can be messy. You know, the accidents and all." He paused again, and she finally understood he was talking about being an EMT. "I guess what I'm saying is, I know when to leave someone well enough alone and when to pull them the hell out of the mess they're in." He coughed slightly and leaned forward with his hands clasped between his knees. "I know what my role is."

He sounded earnest, but this only confused her more. She was trying to talk about their relationship. Why was he discussing work? She suddenly felt extremely tired. The whole thing was beginning to give her a headache.

"Look, Greg, this is almost too much for me to digest. I don't know if I can deal with it right now."

To her irritation, he appeared relieved at this. He stood up and leaned over to kiss her, but she lowered her face and turned away so that he pressed his lips to a reddish-orange curl hanging over her cheekbone. He brushed this lightly with his thick fingers before walking out of the room. Still sitting on the sofa, she wondered, *How did this get turned around?* Greg was like a yo-yo: one moment in the palm of her hand and the next instant flying out of control, beyond her reach.

After dinner, Minnie sat at the table while "her men," as she called them, discussed baseball, Greg in a batter's stance with an imaginary bat in his hands, Bryan cautiously imitating each movement. As she watched them, she was struck by something. Her son was tall and thin, with the awkward joints of a growing boy, where Greg had the confident, compact body of a man who made his living with it, though he didn't overpower Bryan when he was around him, try to crush his fingers in a handshake or talk loudly when they were only a couple of feet apart. The distance between them seemed respectful. But for as well as they got along, Minnie noticed that they didn't touch—not only no crushing handshakes, no handshakes at all, certainly no hugs. She couldn't even remember Greg tousling Bryan's hair.

"Remember, it's all psychological," Greg said. "Don't let them intimidate you. Hang in there at the plate. A curveball only looks dangerous."

"How do I know it's a curveball that's going to curve and not a fastball that's coming right at me?"

"You look for the ball's spin. Anyway, what's the worst that can happen? You get hit, and it hurts. Then you pick yourself up and play on."

"I don't think they should even be throwing curveballs at his age," Minnie said. "I read that they can do permanent damage to their arms before their muscles develop properly."

"Do you want to see my baseball cards?" Bryan asked, still talking to Greg. "I just got a Ken Griffey, Jr. for a Derek Jeter and a Cal Ripken, Jr. for a David Wells. I traded with my friend Jason yesterday. He's a Yankee fan. He doesn't know anything about baseball."

Minnie noticed an arch to her son's eyebrows that she hadn't seen before, and she immediately looked to Greg. He was staring into Bryan's room, but she couldn't read the expression on his face.

"How about if I throw you a few pitches later instead?" he suggested.

"But—" Bryan began and then looked as if he remembered something. "I don't have a ball anymore," he continued. "I lost it in the field behind the park."

"Oh. Well, maybe we can find something else to do. But later, okay?"

Bryan's mouth hung open. Then, shrugging, he snapped it shut and walked into his room, closing the door behind him—not with a slam, but with a force that made Minnie turn and stare into the Ripken "Iron Man" poster as if she might be able to see through it eventually. Greg helped her clear the table, but when she began doing the dishes, he bumped her with his hips until she was out of the way and he stood in front of the sink.

"You've worked hard all day," he said. "I'll take care of these."

"Aren't you the liberated man."

"Who says we haven't come a long way?" He stirred the water with his hands to activate the suds and began vigorously scrubbing a pasta-crusted plate with a steel wool pad. "Speaking of which.

Did you know that in the old TV shows, couples in bed always had to have at least two feet on the floor?"

"Where'd you hear that?"

"I know this guy who studied pop culture in college."

Minnie rolled her eyes but smiled when she remembered that one time against his kitchen sink. Both of *his* feet had been on the floor. "So it was okay for one person to have both feet on the floor and the other to have none?"

Greg squinted at a spot on the plate. "I'm sure the rule was one foot each."

"I wonder," she said, getting into it now, "if the evolution to couples fully in bed was incremental or sudden. I mean, did some shows allow three feet off the floor, or did it go straight from two to four?"

"It had to go straight to four."

When Minnie asked why, Greg seemed slightly exasperated. "Because everybody knows you're doing it once you've got three feet in the air."

Minnie tried to imagine what it would look like, on a bed, but she couldn't get a picture of Mike and Carol Brady out of her head, the first television couple—the first couple, period—she saw in the bedroom together. There was Mrs. Brady sitting primly with the covers folded over her lap, book in hand, but Minnie simply couldn't negotiate Mr. Brady into a coital position without having both of his feet leave the floor, too, unless she dislocated Mrs. Brady from her reading position, which would never happen. This supported Greg's theory about jumping from two to four, but didn't satisfy her desire to visualize three.

"Are you sure about that?" she giggled.

"Believe me, it can be done," Greg returned much more seriously than he needed to. After all, she had only been playing along with him. Why did he have to go and make an inference about some other woman he'd slept with before her? Minnie felt a pang of jealousy and at the same time a pang of inadequacy, as if she should have instinctively known how to make love with three feet in the air, like it was one of the most common positions in the world, right up there with the missionary. So what if she had been a virgin all through high school, up until she got married? Why was he going off and acting so macho all of a sudden?

"It's all about trying something a little different," he continued.

"That's enough!" she shouted, grabbing him by the shoulder and turning him toward her. "This whole thing between us has gone far enough. Is this some kind of weird way to punish me for something?" She looked into his face. "Are you still mad about that stupid parachute thing?"

"I wasn't thinking that, but now that you mention it, it does make sense. You're afraid—"

"Hell yes, I'm afraid. Any sane person would be. The cost of the insurance alone is scary enough. I ought to know."

"You didn't let me finish." He stared past her with his unblinking eyes. "You know, you never told me the last time you took a day off work."

"One of us has to keep both feet on the ground," she retorted. "You're always flying off the handle with these idealistic—I don't know what they are—fantasy quests of yours. Sometimes I don't think you live in the real world."

"And sometimes I don't think you live," he said with equal force.

"You want to live?" she challenged. "Then stay and make love to me tonight, all night long."

"I want to," he said.

"But? There's a 'but' in there somewhere."

"Do you know how much noise we make? What if he walked in on us? It's not right."

"That's bullshit," she was surprised to hear herself say. "This has nothing to do with Bryan. I think you're using this whole issue as an excuse not to get close to me."

The thought had jumped straight from her brain to her mouth, but the look on his face made her certain she had hit the mark. Now, no matter how much she might have wanted to, she couldn't back off, draw him close and comfort him, make him understand it was okay to feel so mixed-up about the idea of an instant family after years of living alone as a bachelor; there was too much momentum behind her words for her to stop.

"In fact, I'm wondering now if all of your life isn't some kind of big dodge. You think you're so brave because you have this dangerous job and do all these dangerous things, but the things that really scare you, you won't go near. And to think," she spoke deliberately now, "I once thought you were a hero."

He clenched and unclenched his fists—helplessly? In anger? She couldn't tell, feeling a little of both herself. Then he turned and walked away. She knew she had hurt him. But rather than making her feel bad, his silence made her glad she had pushed the point.

Greg brought a trampoline over the next day and set it up in Minnie's backyard before she got home from work.

"Well, what do you think?" he asked proudly when she stepped onto the patio. Bryan was already jumping up and down on the new toy.

"Bryan, get down from there!" she said sharply. When he didn't do so immediately, she whipped off her sunglasses and pointed to the ground. The fierceness of her movements combined with the heat made her reddish-orange curls crinkle and sway like flames.

Bryan climbed down from the contraption, but instead of abandoning it completely, he leaned against it while standing next to Greg. They both looked guilty, like two puppies about to be reprimanded for digging up the yard.

"Greg, what are you doing?"

He didn't answer at first, only nodded slightly at Bryan and then hitched his eyes in the direction of the house. When Minnie didn't budge, he said, "After our talk last night, I thought it would be nice if I did something to—you know."

"This is insane. Do you know how dangerous these things are?" She didn't want to, but she couldn't help it: in her mind she saw Bryan in a heap by the trampoline, his arms and legs broken. She shuddered and wondered what she had ever seen in Greg.

"I have a buddy with three kids who has one, and they've never been hurt, not even a little. It's all in how you use the thing."

"Tear it down now and take it back to wherever you got it."

"But I thought it would be fun for Bryan."

"You thought it would be fun for *you*." Minnie stamped a foot. "Bryan said he needed a baseball. I never once heard him mention a trampoline." Her son shifted on his feet, his head hung down, his straight brown hair hiding his eyes, and she felt bad for talking about him as if he weren't standing right in front of her. She also didn't want him to hear the rest of what she had to say. "Honey," she said, "why don't you go into the house for a while?"

Bryan hesitated for a moment and then began to scuffle toward the patio door, kicking at the grass. Before he was out of reach, Greg gave a start, as if he'd been daydreaming and suddenly snapped back to the moment. Then he brought one hand up and placed it on Bryan's shoulder. He held it there for a second and gave a gentle squeeze as if to let the boy know it was okay, everything was going to be okay. Bryan stopped, looked at his mom, and then disappeared inside.

"I'm sorry," Greg said, his hands awkward again, motioning toward the trampoline. "I like Bryan, I really do. A baseball seemed so small. I thought I should do something more. I want to do more." His face shone pink. "I'm new at this. I guess it was a stupid idea."

Minnie felt sick to her stomach. Everything she'd been about to say was stuck in her throat, held there by his words and his gesture.

"You can take this thing down tomorrow," she said quietly. "Right now I just want to be alone."

Ten minutes after he'd left, she sat by herself on the sofa, wrapped in an oversized man's flannel shirt—Greg's—with her knees pulled to her chin, holding a glass of sugarless iced tea. She thought of his hands, hands that had caressed her many times, that had touched death, that had saved lives—sometimes, it suddenly occurred to her, all at once. She'd been handling it all wrong, resisting him when she should have just given him what he wanted, what he said he wanted. Right on Bryan's shoulder— it had looked so paternal. And vulnerable. She felt attracted to Greg in this new position and also vaguely powerful for putting him there. She wanted more of both—his naked honesty and her power—and instinctively knew what she could do to get them.

Minnie phoned Greg two hours later.

"I'd like you to come over," she said. "We need to talk."

"Can't we talk now?" he said, his voice tired.

"No, I'd prefer to do it face-to-face."

He expelled air into the mouthpiece, and it sounded like wind in Minnie's ears. "All right. I've got a long day ahead of me tomorrow, but all right. Wait a minute." She heard items being shuffled on the bureau where he kept his phone. "What time is it? Why aren't you at the gym?"

"Nine o'clock, but it doesn't matter. I took the night off."

"What?"

"I took the night—"

"I heard you, I heard you. I'm just wondering why."

"Come on over and I'll tell you," she said and hung up. While she waited for him to arrive, she rewashed the dishes because they had water stains on them and vacuumed the living room floor a second time. He showed up with his hair in a daze, his face dark with stubble, one end of his shirt hanging lower than the other because he had buttoned the next-to-last button in the last hole and worked up from there.

"I came over as fast as I could," he said. "I got worried—"

"Take off your clothes," she said.

He raised his eyebrows, opened his mouth, closed it.

"Do I have to do it for you?" she asked.

He looked around the house, and when he turned around she was already unbuttoning his lopsided shirt.

"Bryan's sleeping over at a friend's house," she said. "He'll be gone all night."

Greg was naked to the waist now, and she loosened his belt and pulled his jeans down over his hips. Her heart beat wildly in her chest as she unbuttoned her blouse and pulled off her slacks. After stripping to her bra and panties—her sexy pair, made of a satiny red material, and very little of it—she turned and motioned for Greg to follow. She could hardly keep her breath quiet, she was so excited, and then she wondered why she was trying to control it.

"Where are you going?" he asked when she walked past the bedroom and into the kitchen.

"Outside," she said.

Through the patio door he peered at the houses peeking above the fence. "It's not completely dark yet. The neighbors might see us."

Ignoring him, and resisting the urge to smooth out her panties and stop them from riding any higher, she approached the trampoline. The springs around its edges appeared even more dangerous in the fading light, and its flat black surface practically emanated heat. But he looked so uncomfortable in his red plaid boxers and black cotton socks, his broad shoulders tight and hairy arms scrunched protectively at his sides, she knew she had to go through with it, or at least have the satisfaction of letting him talk her out of it. Quickly, before losing her nerve, she stripped bare and mounted the trampoline. The material wasn't as hot as she'd expected. In fact, it felt comfortable, like a second skin. To her surprise, Greg took off his undergarments and climbed up next to her.

"What's next?" he asked softly.

"Make love to me," she said.

The notion was both delicious and ridiculous, and he must have felt the same, too, at first, because it took him a minute to get an erection. But once they had fallen into the sway of joined motion, she forgot her self-consciousness and was surprised to find she was having fun. Smells she had never smelled in this context wafted over her: lilacs, daisies, dusty earth, sweat, and polyester-coated nylon. The sound of an occasional passing car took on a whole new meaning, as did the drone of a lawnmower from somewhere far down the block. She floated in a reverie where every feeling was heightened. As Greg thrust in and out of her, she reached behind her and pushed off from the trampoline to meet him, and they fell into a soft, undulating rhythm. Then she knew she wanted to go even further.

"What are you doing?" he asked.

"Trying to bounce. Go harder." A flush of guilty pleasure filled her face. "Fuck me harder."

They made little leaps off the trampoline's surface, but she could tell his thrusting was fighting the lift she wanted, so she made him slow, stop, and, remaining unmoving while still inside her, push off from the trampoline with *his* hands. At first, they simply squished into the fabric and squished out without really rising from it. Then they made a deeper indentation, then deeper.

Then it happened. They were making love in the air. That's exactly what it was. She was looking right into his eyes, and he was looking back, and though they weren't moving their bodies together, she could feel him sliding inside her with every bounce. And they weren't just falling, they were flying, too—up and down, up and down, first one foot, then two feet, then three feet high. Minnie thought of what her neighbors might see if they looked out their windows right then: a single naked shadow hovering over the top of the fence for a split second before disappearing, hovering and disappearing. There was the safety of a common boundary and then sudden carnality rising above it. The thought made her squeal. She had nothing to hide. When she looked past Greg's face and over his shoulder, all she could see was sky, then the low bulk of her house, and then sky again, swirled in purple twilight, until she closed her eyes and felt only blackness and a dizziness and his arms tight around her, his left hand on her shoulder, his right hand cupping the small of her back, as they slowed and slowly settled again into the pull of the earth.

LITTLE MURDERS

I've never believed in miracles. And I never pray. Wouldn't even know how to begin, really. Sure, I went to church growing up, this clapboard Catholic affair upstate where the aspens turn bright as a circus in the fall, but that didn't have anything to do with God that I could see, even when I was a kid. I cut my deal with heaven, went through confirmation, was baptized, the whole thing, but I never felt a change come over me, like drowning and then having a wave of love save me, never felt different in any way except that I was wet. I had hoped for something more, but when puberty hit me even worse than I'd expected, I realized I didn't have a clue as to what praying was about. My parents weren't too pushy about church or anything, so when I turned eighteen I was free to do whatever I wanted, and that meant no praying.

And anyway, what would I tell her? She's a lot like me—caring, smart, a bit conceited, with many friends and few lasting friendships. The only thing I would consider a miracle is if we could somehow talk to each other.

We did have our baptism, though, and that was sex. It was the only time we could communicate, naked, under water, away from all the social graces that required us to wear our separate lives like masks and different backgrounds like snowsuits in summer. Somehow, when we got past the tired ritual of *How was your day?* and fell into the moment that was our bed, floor, table, or whatever, we found ourselves as if in two different bodies, our new forms not cranky or absorbed with things like investments and utilities. Some of my friends say we couldn't have been that great together since we were never really in love, that it was all in my head, but that's a lie. We understood things that were never spoken, that can't be spoken. I would argue that's more important than just talking sometimes. My friends don't understand because they're all married.

As to our being in love: I don't know what that means any more than I know what praying's about. The only thing that comes close is something someone once said about how sex is like death.

Her name was Mary. Is. She's tall, seems taller than me, but I'm nearly six feet, and when she stands next to me you can see she's a couple of inches shorter, but she has that kind of *stature*, you know what I mean? And there's something ageless about her. Me, I pretty much look my twenty-seven years, baby-faced but with a shock of gray hair from all the stress of working at a bank. I need to get away from that sometimes and into something that makes me feel less counterfeit, so I like going to shows, concerts, things like that. That's where I first noticed her, standing near her while enjoying some wine after Mendelssohn's "Elijah." She had on this simple cotton skirt that came down to just below her knees, showing off her long, slim calves but tight enough to outline her strong thighs. Her skin was olive dark, her hair long, black, and wavy. There was a smell about her, not a perfume but a pleasant odor of some kind that reminded me of my childhood.

But the most fascinating thing about her were her eyes, as dark as brown could get and still be brown.

She stood there for about ten minutes, quietly, as if waiting for someone, though no one came. So when I finished my wine I asked if she wanted to grab a coffee or something, and she said yes. We went to a little shop around the corner and talked; as it turned out, it was our longest conversation. It was almost like we were old friends getting to know each other again before settling back into our comfortable relationship. She reminded me of this older girl I knew from when I went to church, and when I told Mary that she smiled and asked me what this girl was like.

Like you, I said. With eyes, I thought I could swim in. *And her personality?* Mysterious, like she knew a good secret and wasn't telling. *Didn't you ever ask her?*

I was too embarrassed to admit that while I'd tried a few times, I couldn't because I felt so guilty. I couldn't help thinking about us having sex. From when I was about fourteen, I sat in those pews and imagined pulling her into one of the confessional booths, telling her about my fantasies, and having her nod in wide-eyed understanding. Then the two of us would wait for everyone to leave so we could emerge from the booth naked and lie on the altar, the sound of the baptismal font the only sound over us except our own breaths. Or sometimes I would skip all that and go straight to the altar, the two of us joined right there in front of the priests and the choir and the whole congregation, and only afterward would we be married. Those thoughts made me so ashamed I could hardly look her in the eye whenever I tried to say anything to her. I didn't want to tell Mary that no matter how much I prayed it didn't stop those feelings. So I just told her the girl and her family moved away before I got a chance to know her.

I actually wondered for a while if maybe Mary was her, my old childhood crush grown up, but she never let on like she knew anything about the people or places I talked about. She mostly just listened and sipped her herbal tea while I downed my coffee. When I asked her what she did, she said she taught at the private college down in the valley. I told her I never thought I'd be a loan officer, but that I tried to like it, and when I couldn't try anymore I'd pretend. She was the first woman I ever knew who seemed to understand that. We stayed out until two in the morning, and a week later she moved into my house.

She didn't own much: a crate of books, a small bookshelf, half a closet full of the same kind of clothes she had on when I first met her, some gardening equipment, and an assortment of knick-knacks—candles, a set of antique silver candlesticks, a few bundles of incense, a brass incense burner, and a cedar box full of jewelry and beads. Though she also owned a beautiful rosewood picture frame, she didn't have any pictures of her family. When I asked about this she admitted she had one of herself, and I convinced her to set it up in what became our shared bedroom. In the picture she was so beautiful, confident, and serene, she looked like she was glowing.

Now, I've hated most of the jobs in my adult life, but I'd always been able to fake my way through them until I met Mary. Then I found it hard to contain my feelings anymore, even though I tried. After work, I'd pull off my overcoat and hang it up neatly in the closet before turning to give her a peck on the cheek and forcing some chatter. She must have sensed my annoyance, but she never said a word. I could never figure out if she was the most giftedly tolerant person on earth or merely indifferent. Probably indifferent. There's something as alluring as cold metal in a sparkling woman's indifference.

I might have just spent the day buying student loans from some other company, and the vice president might have been riding me because he thought I took some carrying too high a risk. Jesus, I might have wanted to say, that's all banking is anyway, odds and risk, just like the stock market or insurance. I know, because I was an insurance salesman, too, for a while, and it drove me crazy. I might as well have been a dealer in Vegas—it would have been about as fair to my clients. Insurance is legalized, institutionalized gambling. The companies basically place their bets that you as insured will or will not have this or that thing happen to you while you're out driving, owning a house, renting, vacationing, or whatever, but they can't play against an even hand, they want to stack the odds in their favor, or, if they can, eliminate them altogether. What do you think life insurance is? What are the chances you're going to live forever? But people still place their bets.

Obviously, I didn't get along too well with my superiors. They wanted "company people," which near as I can figure it meant no-brainers. It was a lot like going to church in that regard, but a little different. They didn't want dummies; they wanted smart people, responsible people, even good people, you know, ethical or moral or whatever, but they didn't want them to be *too* smart. The kind of people who get good grades in college but can't do their own laundry. Church, well, they'll take anybody with dirty laundry. Just don't tell them how to wash it.

Mary was very open-minded, don't get me wrong; she just didn't have a lot to say. Me, I'm always talking because I've got this thing about thinking maybe a little too much. I watch a lot of movies and draw sometimes and even do things like read poetry because I like to get away from all the crap, you know what I mean? Actuarial tables and flexible interest rates and points on mortgages. It all sounds precise, but there's no precision in that. I'll admit, sometimes I think I'm nuts, but I find more precision in the creek behind my house than in the comfortable little murders of banking. Every now and then I go there, right at dawn or dusk is prettiest, and just sit at the water's edge, and if it's nice out like in the summer dangle my feet in the current. The Douglas firs sort of give this sigh, and I get this feeling of just *being*.

Sometimes Mary would join me, and this is when we'd talk. We never *said* anything, hardly anything, but we'd sit together and sometimes nuzzle close, and like I said, if it was a nice day we'd both have our feet in the water, and pretty soon we'd be naked and rolling in the soft grass there by the bank of the creek. There was a naturalness to it that made it seem we were each other's first lovers. I could have sworn when my seed fell to the earth that Mary would sprout there like wild roses, reaching her petals to the sun, it was like she just kept expanding and I was really deep inside her. I guess I must have lost myself. Or did I prick myself on her thorns and bleed, each drop a bruise-colored petal, a remembrance? Maybe every time we made love a piece of me withered and died, but they bloomed in Mary, and isn't that how nature works? During those moments I couldn't have cared less if usury never existed and I was out of a job. I would have lived right there by the water with her, like two nymphs in a forest. I might have become a poet or an artist even. Who knows?

But afterwards, I could never tell her how I felt; she either didn't think it was important enough to vocalize or was comfortable enough with who she was that she didn't need to romanticize everything like me. What ended up happening was just one of those things that sneak up on you, certainly nothing you can insure yourself against.

Just think about insuring something you've never considered insuring before and you'll suddenly find it becomes more valuable than you'd ever imagined—not only that, but this thing you hardly knew you had suddenly becomes something you can't live without. I saw it often when I sold insurance; they were the people who couldn't buy enough. They were my best customers, but I always felt like talking them out of it, like sending them anonymous refund checks, because I thought I had a conscience. Now I think it was because I was unconscious, that in some deep, imprecise way I knew I was taking Mary for granted.

One morning we were lying by the creek, drinking our coffee and tea like it was breakfast in bed, the scent of sagebrush and pine over us like cool cotton sheets. As I stroked her arms, it suddenly occurred to me I had thirty years to go before I could collect my retirement benefits. For a second I couldn't breathe, like the weight of all that time made the air too heavy. My first reaction was to reach for Mary. I asked her where she saw herself in thirty years.

Don't you even know what I do? she asked with a misty smile, spreading her hands in front of her like she was smoothing an apron with the backs of them. Of course I knew, I already told you, but that wasn't the point. I wanted to know if she *enjoyed* her work, if it was like a teller's line, the same transactions every day, or a creek with grassy banks—sometimes swelling, sometimes drying up, but always moving, never silent, a voice for two people who couldn't talk because they were under water.

We sat watching the sunrise in silence, and at some point she must have gotten up and walked away, because the next thing you know I was alone. When I looked at my watch, I realized I was late for work, so I ran into the house and rushed through shaving and brushing my teeth while at the same time looking for Mary. She wasn't around. I figured she was in the garden she kept behind the woodshed at the far end of the yard, but not having time to kiss her goodbye, I called out the back door instead and went to work.

When I came home that evening, everything looked okay, but the place had the *feeling* of being empty. I felt like I was looking in on someone else's life, like a claims adjustor checking to see what was broken or missing. I started in the bedroom. Her candles and beads were still there, on top of the bookshelf, beside the rosewood picture frame where her picture always was, but the picture was gone. I took a good look around then and could see she had taken most of her things—her books, her clothing, her jewelry, the incense, though the smell of it still hung in the air. Just like at work when I balance the books, it made me want to scream. And for once I did. I swore and howled in my empty little house, just like I had always wanted to at my boss.

Mary! I yelled. Why did you leave me by the water? I didn't get an answer, not even in a note. All I was left with were memories, some candles, and that string of dark beads.

Now, I'm not sure why I did this, but I took those candles and lit them till the wicks burned high and dripped a river of wax right there on the wooden bedroom floor. From memory I dripped a body, then a head, then two mounds in the shape of eyes, and I planted those beads like flowers in their beds. I tried to find some way to talk to her, tried until blood pounded in my head, but the words wouldn't come. She didn't come back. I couldn't bring her back. I sat on the edge of the bed and cried, my nose filled with the smell of wax and phosphorous of burnt matches, covering the smell of her, and I didn't move until the sound of rushing water outside my window melted with the sound of wind and creaking of the house and eventually became so loud I couldn't hear it anymore, it was all one sound and no sound at once. In the end, I had nothing to ask for, nothing to say. I didn't have a prayer. And like I said before, I've never believed in miracles.

GOING FOR BROKE

When the check came to reimburse us for what happened during the war, I was more amused than relieved. Twenty thousand dollars. The average pro baseball player makes over a million dollars a year now. But it can't be helped. These are different times. For me, what happened after the war was more important—one game in particular. It occurred exactly forty-four years ago, in the middle of August 1949, but I can still remember nearly every pitch because there was a major league scout in the stands that day and because after that game, everything would be different.

In many ways it was typical, played against a local all-star team on whatever field we could find, at a high school in Portland in this case. The crowd spilled out of the bleachers and lined the field on either side, women in high heels with umbrellas, men in suits with hats. It reminded me of the time I had spent in the city seven years earlier, people pressed against the fence to see how the Army had us living in horse stalls.

By the fourth inning, I began to realize I was pitching especially well. The first batter in the inning had grounded out; the second struck out swinging. Now I faced their third hitter. That's when I looked up at the scoreboard and saw all those zeros. In baseball, it's bad luck to think about pitching a no-hitter, so I blocked everything out of my mind except what my father had taught me: to remain balanced, in control, prepared for anything. I went into my windup and fired a fastball, landing with my body square to home plate, ready to field a bunt or a line drive. The batter was a tall, blonde kid with thick forearms, but he couldn't get his bat around quickly enough to connect with my pitch.

When Tommy Ishikawa, my catcher, called for a curveball next, I nodded. Not wanting to hang it and let this guy drive it deep, I aimed low, and it tailed away from his swing. As the umpire signaled strike two, someone in the crowd yelled, "Herro, Jap boy!" But I didn't care what he said. I was an American. I reached back and threw so hard the ball smacked into the catcher's mitt and made a noise that echoed off the bleachers. The batter never moved.

The umpire yelled out and jerked his thumb over his shoulder. Tommy pulled off his glove, shaking his hand and rubbing it. I walked off the field and didn't hear a thing the crowd said.

I was the star pitcher on the Nisei All-Stars. I was an American.

I was born November 13, 1927, the year the great Babe Ruth hit sixty home runs. Every morning that summer as I grew in my mother's womb, my father read the sports pages and marveled out loud at the Babe's enormous talent, listening to Yankees games on the radio whenever we could get them in Wapato, Washington, in the heart of the Yakima Valley. Like fallow earth, I accepted the seeds of my father's love of the Yankees and baseball even before I was born.

My father had seen the Babe when he was still a pitcher with the Boston Red Sox and played against the St. Louis Browns on his way to a second twenty-win season. My father never tired of describing the Babe's ferocious curveball, perhaps because the big man later took part in two tours of Japan that helped bring about professional baseball in that country, before the war put everything on hold.

"He would be the best pitcher today if he weren't also the best hitter," my father often told my mother, who became interested in the game when my older brother Frank began playing. Frank was a shortstop like my father, but because I grew quickly, and because of my father's early admiration of the Babe, it was determined that I would be a pitcher. As soon as I could pick up a baseball with both hands, I would roll it to where my father stood only a couple of feet away, and he would slowly back up as I learned to roll it farther and farther. When I could hold the ball in one hand, he taught me to throw, and we would play catch until it was too dark to see.

"The boy is too young," my mother protested. "He is going to get hurt."

"No, *yakyuu* will make him strong," my father said. "It will discipline his body and mind."

Of course, I was told all of this later, after I had indeed grown disciplined and strong because of *yakyuu*—baseball. My father taught me to prepare for a game the same way we prepared our fields for planting every spring, to believe in the manager and adhere to his strategy as part of the natural order of all things. It was the Japanese way.

I am *Nisei*, second-generation Japanese and by birth an American, my parents *Issei*, the first generation, forbidden for years to naturalize. Despite the ocean between them, my father kept in touch with his relatives in Japan, who wrote to him of baseball's growing popularity there. Sitting at our wooden kitchen table with his wire-rimmed reading glasses on, he would sometimes translate for me the strange black markings that arrived on wispy paper in thin envelopes. Their lives did not sound much different from ours: the worry of long days in the fields and fluctuating farm prices, the pleasure of baseball on the weekends. But in many ways, my aunts and uncles and cousins remained as mysterious as the language they wrote in. I'd never met any of them. The Babe's tours were my main connection to my father's country. My heroes were the American players, like Joe DiMaggio and Dizzy Dean, and I never doubted that one day I would become one of them.

Growing up a farm boy during the Depression wasn't as bad as it might sound. As non-citizens, my parents weren't allowed to buy land, but they leased twenty acres on the Yakima Indian Reservation that we kept in potatoes, hops, cantaloupes, and onions. We never seemed to have much money, but we never went hungry, for we also tended a large garden of tomatoes, corn, squash, cabbage, beans, cucumbers, and other vegetables my mother would jar or pickle to keep us through the winter, as well as a flock of chickens and a cow.

Besides being a farmer, my father was a baseball star for the Wapato Nippons, who won the Mt. Adams League pennant in 1934 and '35. But while I admired his strong throwing arm and the way he hit line drives, there were things I didn't understand about him. He talked of how he hoped to become an American citizen, but he still practiced *Búkkyo*, the Buddhist religion of his father. He meditated every morning and evening, waking up even earlier than I did to perform my chores. He never seemed to get very excited about the game I loved, whether he won or lost. Though there was talk he might be recruited to play for the Seattle Asahis in the Nisei Baseball League, I couldn't tell how much he cared.

I looked up more to my only brother, Frank. He was four years older than me, and even more than my father, he wanted to be American—not just legally, which he was, but in every way. He smoked Pall Mall cigarettes and listened to the boogie woogie and big band music of "Lux" Lewis and Benny Goodman, and though I'd never been anywhere outside of the Yakima Valley, I imagined he could swing dance as well as anyone in Portland or Seattle, maybe even St. Louis or New York. He knew all the movie stars by name—Myrna Loy was his favorite—and he would sneak these calendars into the house with color drawings of beautiful American women with very short skirts and tight sweaters, or sometimes no clothes at all.

Whenever we could, usually on a Sunday afternoon when our chores were light and he wasn't with a steady girlfriend, he would drive us into Wapato to watch a movie and then eat a snack at the drugstore and listen to the jukebox. Frank always ordered a vanilla milkshake with an egg broken into it. We had stopped going to Yakima because they wouldn't let us into the theater, saying our clothes were dirty even if we hadn't been in the fields that day. But for the most part, we were treated well in Wapato.

One time, though, when I was about twelve and Frank sixteen, he got into a fistfight with an older boy who insulted us in the street. I was already Frank's five foot seven, but he weighed thirty pounds more and had four extra years of baling straw in his arms.

"What did you say?" he asked loudly so that the other boy, who had passed us, could hear him.

The boy turned around and walked back. He was tall, much taller than Frank, and his gums seemed too loose around his teeth. I watched his face turn from pale to bright pink. "I said go back where you came from," he said. "We don't need you here stealing our jobs."

"I was born in this country same as you," Frank said, squaring his shoulders so that for a moment he looked bigger than he really was.

"Yellow devil," the boy said in a way that seemed he was spitting at us. Without warning Frank punched him in the face and didn't let up, pounding the boy while he stood there, dazed. Blood ran from his nose, and a drop of it spattered onto my good white shirt. I watched it run in a small stripe down my chest pocket before soaking in, and my first thought was that our parents would be angry. When I looked up, the boy lay on the ground, Frank standing over him with both fists.

"Around here, we call cowards yellow," he said.

I forgot all about my shirt then and only wanted to be like Frank—a tough American kid.

We didn't have radar guns in 1949, but I threw as hard as any of the major leaguers. More importantly, I could throw the ball where I wanted it. Going into the bottom of the fifth inning of that game against the local all-stars, I hadn't even allowed a runner to reach base. Finally, with two outs, I walked their shortstop. The crowd cheered like they had just won a pennant.

I was still trying not to think too much about my no-hitter, but I couldn't help looking into the bleachers. Earlier that summer, I had thrown a shutout against the Pacific Northwest League champs, and after the game, my manager pointed out a scout for the Brooklyn Dodgers, a stocky man with dark, curly hair who stuck a notebook in his jacket pocket before disappearing in the parking lot. I couldn't help wondering if he was there among all those screaming fans in Portland. We had been told some scouts might be covering the game—to see the white players, I knew, not my team, but I was pitching so well, I thought I stood a chance of being discovered.

Japanese Americans weren't allowed to play in the major leagues after the war—an unspoken agreement but as binding as a contract—and there were no full-time, professional Japanese American leagues. We got by playing anyone we could—high school and college teams, town teams, other *Nisei* teams. Sometimes we played exhibitions against the Negro League ball clubs, though they didn't last much longer after Jackie Robinson finally reached the big show in 1947.

We were almost the first non-whites to make it. In 1941, Henry Honda, a *Nisei* from San Jose and a pitcher just like me, signed a contract with the Cleveland Indians. Many of us in the Yakima Valley became excited, especially the players and their families. We were working our field when two of my father's teammates, Kenichi Ono and Tsuneo Yasuda, drove up in Kenichi's Plymouth. He jumped out waving a letter from his cousin in California, which he read out loud when my father, Frank, and I joined them.

"Do you know what this means?" Kenichi asked when he had finished reading.

I wasn't yet fourteen, but I knew. Someone from our culture had made it. My father, though born overseas, could now show that the seeds he had sown in his new country had taken root and grown deep. He stood with his hands in the pockets of his overalls. Tsuneo reached out and grasped him by the shoulder.

"Perhaps Joe will be next," he said. "Everyone is talking about how good he is already."

My father didn't look at me. Instead, he pulled out his right hand and placed it on Tsuneo's shoulder, and the two men stood connected like that for a moment. My father's face showed no emotion.

"We will see," he said. "We will see."

But when he pulled his hand away, I could see it was shaking.

Henry Honda never played an inning in the major leagues. On December 7, 1941, a Sunday, the Japanese bombed Pearl Harbor. They might as well have burned our family farm.

Frank and I were drinking milkshakes at the drugstore in Wapato when the news came on the portable Zenith that always sat on the shelf above the blenders. Everyone in the place became quiet, but the soda jerk turned up the radio anyway. Frank quickly pulled some money from his shirt pocket and placed it on the counter.

"Come on, let's go," he said. "We're done now." When I tried to finish the last of my milkshake, he took it from my hands and set it down. "Didn't you hear me? I said we're done." He looked at me hard. Everyone turned to watch us as we put on our jackets, and I felt their eyes burning into our backs as we left.

The next time we drove by that store, a sign hung in the front window: "No Japs Wanted." Other stores where we had shopped and socialized put up similar signs. Just like that, people who had been our friends and neighbors and co-workers became distant strangers or even vocal enemies. It was like being born a second time, only in a foreign land, with different stories in my ears.

It's an irony in life that sometimes our most trying times open doors to greater experiences, like threshing wheat to strip away the coarse husks and get to the sweet kernels of grain. It's an even greater irony that sometimes it doesn't work this way at all, that the trying times signal an end to a way of life and the beginning of a long exile. I never wanted to leave our family farm in the heart of Central Washington's most fertile valley, the only place I had ever called home. *Shikata ga nai*, was all my father said. It can't be helped.

Everything happened fast, and the uncertainty of our situation made it seem to move faster. Within a week of Pearl Harbor, my parents' bank account was frozen. Frank, now eighteen and with his own bank account, could withdraw money only if he showed his birth certificate. That didn't last long, but then my parents had to turn in our radio at the Wapato Police Station and register at the post office as enemy aliens.

In February, as we prepared for the new growing season, we heard rumors that we would be evacuated into the interior of the country. A month later, a man from the Farm Security Administration told us they would watch our farms and equipment.

Taking advantage of sacrifice prices wouldn't be tolerated, he said. It would be considered un-American. But it happened all over the place. Kenichi Ono had just invested $125 in his 1936 Plymouth and only got $25 for it. Tsuneo Yasuda, who had been among the first settlers in the valley to transform the sagebrush desert into a garden, received a third of what his Allis Chalmers tractor was worth. We simply stored our tractor and truck and potato digger in the barn and housed our animals with the Cavanaughs, a white family up the road who seemed sympathetic.

In late May, when we should have been watching our hops vines spiraling clockwise toward the sun, the Army sent in an artillery unit to oversee the relocation of all Japanese Americans in the Yakima Valley, including non-aliens, as they called citizens like my brother and me. Suddenly we had less than a week to prepare for our leaving. We were told we could only bring what we could carry. We wouldn't be allowed to harvest our crops, and plowing them under would be considered sabotage.

On the last day of the month we were "processed" in the Wapato Junior High School gymnasium, where I had gone to school. Other *Nisei* helped by acting as clerks. Everyone was civil, including the artillerymen. Though they looked fierce with their guns and green fatigues, they were kinder than most of our white neighbors had been since the bombing. One soldier, a corporal named Joe, treated my friends and me especially well, sneaking us chocolate bars and showing us magic tricks, such as making a coin disappear from his hand and then reappear behind his ear. He smiled and mussed the hair on our heads. He said he had an uncle, a businessman, who had visited Japan on a steamship in the 1920s and brought back stories that didn't sound anything like the letters my father read to me, stories of busy market streets, exotic colors and smells, and the most beautiful, polite people on earth. Corporal Joe himself had always hoped to visit one day, and now he was afraid he was going to get his wish.

Less than a week later, my family and I were loaded on a train bound for Portland. People clutched suitcases full of clothes but also crates of books or heirloom China, typewriters, lamps, cooking pots. My mother brought an assortment of sewing tools, my father his Buddhist shrine. Frank brought his collection of big band records, though we had to leave the phonograph behind. I, naturally, took my baseball equipment. I still believed in the future then, still held onto my father's dreams I had soaked up in my unborn sleeping. Very slowly, though, I woke up and learned to believe what my eyes saw before me.

The Army had called in the infantry to help herd us onto the train. Kenichi Ono's family was ahead of where we stood in line on the platform. An infantryman poked Mrs. Ono in the arm, causing her to drop a framed picture she carried. The glass shattered as it hit the ground, ruining the frame, but Kenichi bent over to retrieve the picture. When he did so, the infantryman shoved him, almost knocking him down.

"Giddyup there, Old Paint!" the infantrymen said, laughing. He looked around to see if his buddies had heard him, and they laughed, too. He then kicked away the picture and its broken frame. "You won't be needing that at the glue factory."

Several others were rough as well, and the artillerymen, who had watched over us for a week and a half, wore tight faces. Some began muttering their disgust so that we could hear them. The infantryman who had shoved Kenichi boarded the train and began directing people, grabbing them by their arms and pushing them into the first open seats, whether or not they were near their loved ones. When Kenichi and his wife became separated, he protested. The soldier laughed again, though this time without his mocking smile.

"My, my, the horsey talks," he said. "Might have to put a bridle and bit on this one."

My family was already seated, but I remained standing in the doorway to the car, clutching my baseball mitt to my chest. The artilleryman I knew as Corporal Joe moved past me and up to the other man. Both wore identical stripes on their sleeves.

"You're out of line," Corporal Joe said. "Me and my boys don't like what's going on."

"Maybe you should mind your own damn business."

"Watch your mouth. There are women and children here."

"I won't have you telling me what to do." He shoved Corporal Joe's shoulder, and Joe pushed back with both hands. They grabbed each other's shirts and began wrestling, each trying to gain an advantage, before falling into an empty seat, the infantryman's feet slipping out from under him. Corporal Joe jerked the man up and smacked him hard, sending his head through the window. There was the crash of glass and the faint tinkling of pieces hitting the platform, an excited sound like rain among the soldiers. All of us remained completely silent, though Frank stood up in his seat, his forearm muscles clenching and unclenching.

Later, sometimes, I would think of Corporal Joe when I pitched, the ball a coin that disappeared before the batter could hit it. I would think of Frank, something in me rising, causing me to feel taller than I really was.

In the bottom of the sixth, their leadoff batter got their first hit of the game. He lined it hard into left field, and after he saw that he couldn't stretch it into a double, he hustled back to first base and clapped loudly. Again the crowd became noisy, pressing the field, and I could almost feel their heat against me.

Then I saw him, the Brooklyn scout, leaning forward with his elbows on his knees, expectant, like a catcher calling signals. It was definitely him, the same curly hair, the same notebook in his pocket. The runner on first took a big lead, but I didn't think he would try to steal, especially on the first pitch. He did, taking second base easily, and I was angry at myself for letting my guard down. I was thinking too much about the scout and not enough about the game at hand.

The next batter hit a fly ball to right field, too shallow for the runner on second to tag up. He then tried to take a big lead, but I held him close, stepping off the mound several times and once throwing in his direction. Some in the crowd booed, but I didn't care. The man at the plate worked the count full before I struck him out.

Then the tall, blonde kid with thick forearms came up again. My first two pitches were good fastballs on the outside corner, and he missed one and fouled the other away. With two quick strikes on him, I should have backed off and thrown an off-speed pitch, but I came at him with another fastball. It hung a little, and he lofted it high into the air. For a moment, it stood out against the American flag flying above the scoreboard in center field, one large star blotting out the background of other stars, before it fell into my center fielder's glove near the fence to end the inning.

In Portland, we were held on the Pacific Livestock Exposition grounds, where the Army had converted horse stalls into apartments by dividing each stall into two rooms with a swinging door and throwing up a coat of whitewash. The floor was covered with two inches of dust when we moved in. My mother immediately took charge and directed everyone, including my father, to clean the place up. As we did, we discovered that underneath the dust, linoleum had been laid directly over manure-covered boards and that everything had been whitewashed with the walls—spikes and nails sticking out, spider webs, horse hair, hay. We slept in individual folding cots on straw mattresses. There were no private toilets, only public latrines; no fresh eggs, fish, or vegetables, nothing like my mother's *okonomiyaki*, fried batter pancakes she made with cabbage, onion, and beef, only long mess hall lines for Army rations, though rice was served once a day. We lived like this for three months until we were again shipped by train to the Heart Mountain internment camp in Wyoming.

The shades were drawn on our railroad car the entire trip. When we finally arrived at a siding—no station house, only a platform—we stepped off and gathered our baggage, the sun behind us rising over farmland, revealing broad stripes of darkness in the desert in front of us: row upon row of barracks covered in heavy black tar paper. Our new home was set on a flat, treeless bench surrounded by sagebrush and buffalo grass, a barbed-wire fence and eight guard towers. Behind it, to the northwest, a squared-off, eight-thousand-foot peak loomed over the high desert like another guard tower. Heart Mountain.

We had been forced to trade our two-bedroom frame house with a fruit cellar and an attic for a sixteen-by-twenty-foot room. When we first moved in, it was furnished with a stove, a droplight, and four steel Army cots with mattresses. As before, my mother took over arranging the room into a livable space. She pushed two cots together into a corner to form her and my father's marriage bed, partitioning it off with curtains she sewed and hung herself. She scavenged wood that she directed my father to build tables and shelves from, and potted plants that she patiently coaxed into bloom. The camp was composed of more than 450 barracks, each exactly alike, divided into twenty blocks by unpaved streets. The nearest toilet was over a hundred feet from our room.

My father worked hard at what my mother asked of him but showed little interest in the rest of camp life. When over a thousand men left on work release to help with the fall harvest nearby and in southern Montana, my father stayed behind. Instead of topping sugar beets, he squatted in the dirt street for hours and caught my pitches. We never spoke of the war or our situation, only *yakyuu*. He often nodded and muttered, "Good, good," or shook his head and said, "No, like this," correcting me on some mechanical aspect of my pitching. Clouds of dust rose under our feet, and the wind peppered us with small pebbles. We played together like this many nights until the cold became too much and the high-powered searchlights clicked on and began sweeping the fence line between guard posts. Then we would go to our room, chilled to the bone, covered in dust.

I followed the World Series in our camp newspaper, the *Heart Mountain Sentinel*, as the Cardinals beat the Yankees four games to one in St. Louis and New York. Though it was only the first week of October, it had already grown too bitter in northern Wyoming for my father and me to play.

I was five foot nine when I entered Heart Mountain at the age of fourteen. I never grew another inch. Five foot nine was short for a power pitcher even in those days, but I was fast. My father taught me how to use my whole body when I pitched—how to use my windup to generate energy, to gain power from my legs as well as my right arm, to keep myself centered.

I did sit-ups and push-ups every day, ran sprints up and down D Street in every season but winter, and my skinny boy's frame filled out to 170 pounds. My father found a discarded tire, and propping it up against a backstop he made of scrap lumber, he watched me throw through the ring over and over, retrieving each toss. Eventually, I could hit my target nine times out of ten from sixty feet, six inches away—the distance of the pitcher's mound to home plate.

At the camp high school, I made friends more slowly. I began hanging out with Harry Okagaki more than the others, partly because he was smart and a good second baseman, and partly because I was sweet on his sister, Sue. I saw them both often as my parents became good friends with Mr. and Mrs. Okagaki, who had been farmers also, in California.

Once, Mr. Okagaki joked that we might all stay there permanently, like Indians on a reservation, and he and my father laughed. It made me sad, thinking of the reservation lands we had leased and left behind. When my father and I were alone in our apartment, I asked him why he and the other *Issei* seemed to be taking this experience lightly.

"In all the time since I came to America, I never had more than a day off work," he said, smiling widely. "Here, it is like having a vacation for the first time."

"Harry doesn't see any difference between this and what the Nazis are doing," I protested, confused. "He says we should stand up to the government and fight."

My father didn't say anything for a long time, and when he finally did, he looked at the curtains my mother had stitched from mismatched scraps of cloth, pale purple orchids dividing one-half of the room, Scotch plaid the other.

"When one loses something, it makes one angry and want to fight. But when one loses everything…" his voice trailed off, and he cleared his throat. "Then what is there to fight for?"

After my no-hitter was over, the guys all relaxed and slapped me on the back and shoulders, telling me what a good game I was pitching. Their pitcher had scattered several hits by then, but the game was close, and most of the crowd had stayed to watch and curse and cheer.

Tommy called for mixing up my pitches and speeds for their leadoff hitter. After seeing fastballs all game, his timing was thrown completely off when I tossed him two slow curves. I then threw him a fastball to keep him honest and followed it up with a changeup. He was so eager to hit it out of the ballpark that he overswung and hit a pop-up that our second baseman swallowed up. I thought I would try the same thing with their second hitter, but this time, my changeup just floated up there—it had no movement at all—and he clubbed it deep into left-center field. By the time our center fielder came up with the ball and fired it back to the infield, their batter stood on second base. I intentionally hit the next batter between the shoulder blades on the first pitch. He glared at me for several seconds before spitting in the dirt and jogging to first base. I now had a chance to force them into a double play, but still angry at myself for giving up the double, I couldn't settle for a ground ball, I wanted to keep them from touching the ball at all. Their next two batters both struck out.

As I walked off the mound, I noticed for the first time that my pitching shoulder felt sore, but I went right past my manager on my way to the bench without saying anything. I didn't want him to think I couldn't handle it. I had already struck out eleven, but we still only led 2-0, and I was determined to go for broke.

Late in January 1943 it was announced that a special combat unit would be opened up to those who passed a loyalty examination, which all *Nisei* seventeen and older were asked to fill out. For many, questions twenty-seven and twenty-eight were troublesome:

Are you willing to serve in the armed forces of the United States wherever ordered?

Will you swear unqualified allegiance to the United States of America and faithfully defend the United States from any and all attack by foreign or domestic forces, and forswear any form of allegiance or obedience to the Japanese Emperor, or any other foreign government, power, or organization?

My friend Harry and I argued a lot over this, as he was seventeen and I almost so. The worst time was right after Frank became one of the first in camp to complete his questionnaire and volunteer.

"Why should we swear loyalty to a government that's made us prisoners in our own country?" Harry asked. "They're treating us like shit."

He wasn't the only one who felt this way. Some in camp had even asked to be repatriated to Japan, especially many of the *Kibei*, who were born in the U.S. but schooled in Japan. They forgot that

124

the Japanese were the enemy. When I told Harry so, he spat and scuffed the spittle into the ground.

"The United States government is the enemy," he said.

"We're citizens of the United States," I reminded him, repeating what Frank had told me.

"This place we're at now," Harry said, pointing at the machine gun in the guard tower above us, "does it seem like America to you?"

"We won't be here forever," I said. "We should try to make the best of it."

"I am, by not taking that damn examination. When your time comes, you shouldn't, either, instead of going along with it like your brother."

"My brother," I said, my voice rising, "wants to fight for the rights of all of us. He's not willing to just stand around and do nothing."

"Well, *I'm* not willing to lift a finger for Uncle Sam until they give me back my rights."

"You're just making it harder on yourself. These questions are meaningless."

"They're trying to trick us. If we answer yes to twenty-eight, then they'll say that proves we were loyal to the emperor in the first place."

After a long protest, all the *Nisei* registered by the end of March. Harry, like many, gave qualified answers to questions twenty-seven and twenty-eight, writing "yes, when my rights as a citizen are restored" for both. In August, he was sent with nine hundred others to the Tule Lake camp in California, where the Army sent all the "trouble makers." His mother, father, and sister, who had written unconditional yes's on a similar questionnaire, decided to go with him rather than break the family apart. I never saw them again.

I deeply missed the Okagakis, especially Harry and Sue, but

my loyalty remained where it had to, with my family: my mother, who made sure I kept up my studies and excelled in school as well as baseball. My father, who squatted in the dust for hours to catch my pitches without complaining. And Frank, who had joined the Army to show everyone what a hell of a fighter and good American he was. By then he was in Camp Shelby, Mississippi, training with the 442nd Regimental Combat Team, a unit composed entirely of Japanese Americans.

For me and many others in camp, our only chance for escape was *yakyuu*. We called game days B.B.C. Days—Baseball Crazy Days. The *Issei* were especially B.B.C. While it was common to hold raffles or pass around a hat after games, the *Issei* donated the most. At some camps, like Gila River, they raised enough to fund bus trips for their team to play ours. Many even bet on games.

My mother got together with other Heart Mountain War Mothers to put their worry to good use by outfitting our team, sewing uniforms out of mattress ticking and carefully saving flour to mark the batter's box and foul lines on the field. My mother had learned a lot about the game and could talk strategy now, such as when to hit to the opposite field or sacrifice to move a runner up. My father helped recruit and organize the team and a small crew of umpires. He turned down an offer to coach but continued to train me.

Baseball in the camp did something no other experience during the war could: it brought out the fire in both of my parents. When they watched me play, they were able to show the emotion I often felt but otherwise rarely saw.

"Great pitch, Joe! But remember to follow through!"

"That was smart hitting! Way to go with the pitch!"

"Run it out, run it out!"

My father even swore, the only time I ever heard it from him: "Open your damn eyes, ump!" Or, "That was a hell of a game."

Ironically, it was while playing that I found my own quiet space within. I still couldn't understand my father's Buddhism, but I began to see that pitching was like prayer or meditation for me. It was like planting within the seasons. It was a natural thing. *Kokoroyama*, I started calling the pitcher's mound. Heart Mountain. Raised fifteen inches off the ground, it was enough to give me an alpine advantage over my opponents, like a sniper in a high place.

Some of the men in our camp were good ballplayers; like my father, they had starred on Japanese American teams before the war. But they couldn't hit me. For the first time, I understood my power. If I thought of Frank or Harry or Sue, I became nervous, acted like a boy, but on the baseball diamond I could beat grown men at their own game. Rather than relying on my fielders behind me, I could force hitters to make outs by throwing the ball by them. And that's what I did, game after game, sometimes pitching both ends of a doubleheader, all through the summer, through the World Series, as the Yankees beat the Cardinals this time four games to one, and beginning again the next spring.

Around this time, internees who were cleared based on their answers to the loyalty questionnaire were encouraged to leave Heart Mountain for good, though they still couldn't go back to their homes, they had to settle elsewhere. Because of this, my father and mother refused, instead remaining in camp as most of the others did.

One afternoon late in the summer of 1944, one of the administrators who had become close friends with my father, a man I knew as Mr. Franklin, came over to our apartment, accepting my mother's usual offer of tea but refusing my father's challenge to a game of Go. I lay on my cot and pretended to study algebra while listening to them.

"Thank you, Mrs. Suguro," Mr. Franklin said when my mother handed him and my father each a steaming cup and set the pot on the table between them. I think my father knew what was coming, though he waited patiently for his friend to speak.

"I won't beat around the bush," Mr. Franklin said. "You know you've been cleared to leave the center. Officially, we're encouraging as many people as we can to do so. Personally, I think you should. Uncle Sam will even provide transportation to your destination and a little pocket money besides."

"Sounds like prisoners being paroled," my father said slowly.

"I'm serious," Mr. Franklin said. "You know how I feel about this whole situation, but you're not prisoners here, at least not anymore. You can resettle anywhere you want—outside of the restricted Pacific defense zone, of course."

"Wapato is in that zone."

"Yes, it is. But the country is much larger than Wapato."

My father's voice was quiet, but it carried great finality. "We will wait here until the end of the war."

"Listen." Mr. Franklin leaned forward on his chair and rubbed his hands together. "My sister and brother-in-law live in St. Louis. I've already written them a letter and talked with them over the phone. They'd be happy to let you stay with them until you can find some work and a place of your own to live. The city's begging for labor right now because of all the boys who are overseas."

My mother, who had been scrubbing the top of our coal-fired stove, wiped her hands on a towel and walked behind where my father sat.

"We have our own boy overseas," she said.

"Yes, I know," Mr. Franklin said quietly. He took a sip of tea. "How about it? No one knows how long this war will last. It's better than staying here."

"So we won't find in St. Louis what we see here?" my father asked, referring to the "No Japs Allowed" signs that had appeared in the neighboring towns of Powell and Cody.

"I can't promise you that," Mr. Franklin said. "But people are starting to change their minds. A lot of *Issei* like you have bought war bonds, Matsuo, and folks like that. It says something to them, and so does all your hard work and the way you've put up with this situation so well. And men like your son…" He glanced at my mother and then back at my father. "Look, if you don't mind my saying, they're getting some terrific press for the job they're doing fighting the Nazis."

The newspapers and newsreels were full of praise for the 442nd Regimental Combat Team, whose motto was "Go for Broke." The news was often many weeks behind, and in his letters, Frank wasn't allowed to tell us exactly where he was, but we and the rest of the country knew this much—he and his fellow soldiers were some of the best in Europe.

"But I'll be blunt," Mr. Franklin continued. "Good press or no, now or later, you'll be more welcome in the Midwest than you will in the West."

"Everything I ever worked for my whole life is back on my farm," my father said. "I am willing to wait." My mother put a hand on his shoulder, and he reached up and touched it. "We are willing to wait."

My mother turned again to the stove while my father leaned back in his chair and smacked both hands to his thighs. "So, Bob, what are you doing tomorrow afternoon?"

"My wife and I had talked about going to Powell," Mr. Franklin said, sounding flustered. "She wants to buy some seeds for her flower garden."

"You should stay and watch my son Joe pitch. It's a B.B.C. Day."

"No," Mr. Franklin muttered, "it's just crazy. These are crazy days." He set his empty cup on the table. "Tell you what, I'll think about sticking around for the game. You think about leaving, okay?" He picked up his hat. "Thank you again for the tea, Mrs. Suguro."

ℬ

During our turn at bat in the eighth inning, we had scored another run, so we now led 3-0, but I still didn't feel comfortable letting up. A couple of mistakes and one swing of the bat, and they would be right back in the game.

The first batter hit a weak groundball to my first baseman, and the second struck out swinging, but then my catcher made an uncharacteristic error. After I struck out the next batter, Tommy let the third strike pop out of his glove, and by the time he had chased it down, the batter was safe at first.

I saw my manager stand and walk to the end of the bench; a moment later Hank Miwa, a left-hander, started warming up. I don't think our manager was as worried about me as he was about the two left-handed hitters they had coming up. But back in those days, starting pitchers were expected to complete their games, and for me, it was especially a matter of pride that I did so. That Brooklyn scout was in the stands.

That's when the tall, blonde kid came up again. After how deep he had hit the ball his last time up, I was determined not to throw him too many fastballs, since that's what a power hitter likes best. Tommy called for a mix of off-speed pitches and curves, and I agreed, keeping them low. The blonde kid took a golf swing at the first pitch and missed. Then he settled down and let the next three go by, two for balls, one on the outside corner for a strike. The count was now two and two, which meant it was time for my best pitch. I gave it to him.

But this fastball got away from me, and it hung—not much, but it came in at his waist, and he turned and connected like he had been waiting for it all his life. The ball went sailing into left-center field, but I knew this one wasn't coming back down into my fielder's glove. It cleared the chain link fence by twenty feet and landed another fifty feet behind it, bouncing in the gravel parking lot and rolling all the way to the school.

130

The score was suddenly 3-2, but they acted like they had just won the game. The whole team greeted this kid at home plate, and the crowd was jumping up and down in the bleachers. I looked at the Brooklyn scout, but he remained sitting without an expression on his face, writing in his notebook.

So when the next batter stepped to the plate, I decided to shake off almost any call that wasn't a fastball. My arm was very sore now, heavy and numb, but I knew I would have to ice it down after the game as usual anyway, so I just did what I had to and forgot all about the pain, striking out the hitter on three pitches. When I thought of my brother Frank and what he had gone through, it made my job easier.

In one of his letters to me, Frank wrote that the 442nd got their motto from the Hawaiian *Nisei* in his unit. It was pidgin English used by some of the island dice-rollers to mean "go all out." Frank wrote this only to me and not in any of the letters he sent my parents because he didn't want them worrying that he had begun gambling.

Then Frank's letters stopped coming. We learned from the Army that he had earned a Purple Heart; later, another soldier, a corporal like Frank, returned to camp on leave and filled us in on the details. While fighting in Italy, Frank was hit in both ears by shrapnel from an exploding shell. He spent six weeks in a field hospital, and his hearing still wasn't perfect when he faked his way through an exam so he could rejoin his unit. He was with them when they liberated the small village of Bruyers in Southern France after three days of fighting, and shortly after when they saved the Lost Battalion.

These men had become cut off from the rest of their regiment in the dense woods of the Vosges Mountains. They were surrounded by Germans. Mines were everywhere. It took Frank and his men another three days of fighting with grenades and bayonets before they could make their rescue.

It's hard for me to talk about this.

Frank was shot again while leading a charge up the ridge that had originally been the objective of the Lost Battalion. Sometimes I wonder if he even heard it coming, but I suppose it doesn't really matter, the things bullets say. He was posthumously awarded the Distinguished Service Cross for his actions and sent home in a flag-draped coffin. That may have been the only decent thing the United States government did for us. While we were living in tar-paper shacks with corrugated tin roofs and playing baseball in homemade uniforms, Frank slept quietly under polished wood and bright, crisp stars and broad stripes.

My brother is an American hero.

By the middle of 1945, we were loaded up on the trains again, this time to leave for our homes in the West. After living at the camp for so long, it was hard saying goodbye to the many *Issei* and *Nisei* friends we had made, and to the little *Sansei*—third-generation Japanese Americans, 550 born behind barbed wire. As we were packing, Mr. Franklin and his wife visited us one last time and tried to give us fifty dollars.

"It's not from the government, it's from us," Mr. Franklin said. My father refused, though they shook hands while my mother and Mrs. Franklin exchanged kisses. I walked out to the baseball diamond and stood on the mound one last time. I looked at the wasteland of tar paper and desert around me, at Heart Mountain in the distance. Then I yelled as loudly as I could. Then I cried.

As I already mentioned, we had left everything on the farm. We didn't have much, but it was all gone when we finally returned, even our animals. The Cavanaughs, the neighbors we had trusted, wouldn't tell us what had happened, wouldn't talk to us at all. In some of the businesses in Wapato and Yakima, many of the hateful signs were still up or replaced with new ones. Our house was full with Frank's absence. There was nothing for us there. *Shikata ga nai.*

So my mother and father moved to St. Louis after all, she taking a job as a seamstress, he a lathe operator, neither's hands ever to work the soil again. I moved from the valley but stayed in the region to play baseball. Several years went by before I rejoined my parents.

I nodded at the signal from Tommy calling for a fastball and then stared hard at the batter. He didn't move, so I waited a second more until I saw him nervously twist the handle of his bat and rub the dirt in the batter's box with his left foot. Then I looked to the runner at first before firing toward the plate. The batter swung and missed.

The runner, on base from only my second walk of the game, had taken a very big lead. I threw over there a couple of times to keep him close and then nodded at my catcher again. I threw another fastball, but the batter connected with this one and sent it sailing far down the left field line before it curved foul into the crowd standing several rows deep beyond the end of the bleachers. I became angry at myself for throwing the ball over the middle of the plate like that. My next pitch was yet another fastball, high and inside. I imagined it was a hand grenade. The batter nearly fell over trying to get out of the way.

"Watch it, Jap!" he yelled, pointing his bat at me. I took the ball back from my catcher like I hadn't heard a thing. The runner on first took an even bigger lead, but I didn't bother keeping him close this time. The game was over. The runner took off as I reared back and threw as hard as I could, sending it low and away. The batter flailed at the pitch and missed completely. Four fastballs, three strikes.

The batter slammed his bat to the ground and started arguing with the umpire, waving his arms at me, and then my teammates were around congratulating me. I had lost my shutout but allowed only three hits and struck out fifteen, making outs when I needed them the most. It's hard to pitch much better than I did, so I looked for the scout from Brooklyn. After all, this was at least the second time that he had seen me pitch so well.

He stood and tucked the notebook into his jacket pocket and walked out onto the field. But instead of approaching me, he walked up to the kid who had hit the home run and began talking with him. The scout put his two fists together as if holding a bat and took an imaginary swing; he then shielded his eyes with his right hand over his brow as if watching something sail far, far away. The blonde kid laughed and looked down. The scout nudged him, and the kid laughed again and made a muscle with his forearms. The scout gave them a good squeeze and then slapped the kid on his back before the two turned and walked together toward the school beyond the fence.

I knew then that I would never pitch in the major leagues. I just stood on the mound and watched them until they were gone. It couldn't be helped. There was nothing I could do.

Some people in the crowd started yelling, or I finally heard them, every word, it seemed, as if there were cowardly devils scratching at my ears. "You got lucky, Jap," shouted one voice. "You're not wanted here," came another. "Why don't you go home?" I simply walked off the field with my head up. They could say whatever they wanted. When I pitched, I was more than a ballplayer. When I wore a Nisei All-Stars uniform, they were the enemy, and they would not win.

THE CAT PEOPLE

And so it was that the cat people came and carefully followed every cat and marked how well they were treated by humans, and, so watching and judging, saved some people and destroyed many others, and in that manner was decided the fate of the world.

Wilma Shoemaucher, age forty-two, a little round knitting shop owner in Beaverton, Oregon, with thick glasses and long brown hair and a propensity to laugh a little too loud at her own jokes, which sometimes caused unease in others though she was otherwise attentive and kind, was spared. And the cat people came with whiskers twitching and appointed her Minister of Finance in the new regime.

And two acne-scarred boys living in Great Falls, Montana, though they were each just thirteen and only had the examples of their uneducated and abusive nuclear families to model, were killed on the spot where they stood by the local chain frozen treats emporium, holding a watermelon slushy and a peanut butter cup sundae, respectively, in their hands when the cat people came with their bodies like humans and heads and tails like cats.

Ralph Mason was an amiable man, a soft-spoken fellow who for fifty-three years faithfully attended Our Holy Mother Virgin of the Sanctified Bleeding Heart Catholic Church in Topeka, Kansas. He tithed every Sunday, just under 10 percent—he always rounded down, unable to bear giving an uneven amount and equally loathe to give over 10 percent—and was unusually tidy in his appearance. He was never a member of the choir during his membership in the church, which commenced with his baptism as an infant, owing to a particularly nasal tone in his singing voice, a carryover from his speaking voice, but pound for pound he sang with unequaled gusto with anyone in the church, not quite as loud as Ethyl Marmot, but she had fifty pounds on his 150-pound frame. Proportionally his voice was just as loud, and, despite the unpleasant twang, at least he could sing in tune. Despite his habit of combing his thinning hair in a severe swoop over his balding head to cover the remarkably pink and shiny scalp exposed there, he was a handsome man, his eyebrows like thick crescent moons with the convex sides facing up, an aquiline nose so perfectly curved he could have been directly descended from the Romans without any cross-breeding with barbarian tribes, and a firm oval face that looked a good three or four years younger than his fifty-three, with the blue-gray of his razor stubble an even, impeccably close-shaved wash over his face and neck, the bottom half of his head not given to the mange that had afflicted his top.

And yet, this quiet, handsome, somewhat tight-pursed man was irksome and peevish at home, and occasionally, in fits of distemper, he would kick his cat, a large, six-year-old female tabby with stripes the colors of pumpkin and ivory, whenever she would get under his feet while he was fixing dinner or precariously balancing it upon the TV tray he used to transport his victuals into the sunken family room, which is what he called it since that's what he'd been told it was when he bought the three-year-old split-level back in 1980, even though he had no family. And because of this indiscretion, the cat people stabbed him through the heart with his own fireplace poker, one he had never used before because it was ornamental, like his fireplace, and the cat people dragged him out back and propped him underneath a flaming maple, the only tree he had planted the entire time he had lived there, and under which several minutes later he died.

The cat people were neither cats nor people. They were aliens. They possessed many of the best and worst qualities of both cats and humans, however. From the humans they took the form of the lower half of their bodies. From human minds they took scientific reasoning, a straightforward, logical approach to thinking with little regard for aesthetics or artistic proportion unless those were also related to science. To the cat people, logic was art; symmetry and balance as found in those motions and lines that could be backed with mathematical equations constituted the highest form of art. They detested free forms of any kind. When they wrote poetry, it was strictly metered and rhymed, and the themes were always practical ones relating to science, politics, mathematics, architecture, or other technical concerns. When they created art, it was always based on lines, curves, and angles that clearly could be shown to relate to a motion in nature. Colors were always chosen for their relation to each other on the color wheel. Subjects were always based on objects and situations in the world and never along more rubbery, elastic, ethereal slants, such as dreams or fantasies. In fact, they rarely indulged in poetry or art at all except as a form of diversion, and in this sense they played. They didn't—couldn't—conceive of photography as art. Photography was useful only insofar as it accurately depicted an event or person, and subjective tools such as framing, lighting, and special developing or matting techniques weren't considered because they were unheard of. A good photograph clearly showed a person, place, or event as it was or had happened, and anything else was simply discarded as trash.

From the cats the cat people took their heads and tails and many of the instincts and ways of thinking like a cat. Like cats, the cat people lived in each moment. They had no sense of irony or sarcasm or other forms of wit; their wits were lightning instincts, an ability to assess a situation immediately and pounce upon it or delicately wait with tails twitching. They felt fear when fearful, annoyance when annoyed, anger when angry, joy when joyful, hunger when hungry. They had no sense of time in the future. They looked at the world alert and vigilant, and the world was exactly as they saw it. Like both cats and humans, they were intelligent. The sense of play they inherited from cats was a spontaneous kind, born of the moment, and they could make use of whatever medium they had at hand to produce enjoyment. Like cats, they sometimes became bored just as quickly, and they were often prone to taking long naps in the sun. Thus, despite their brilliance, they didn't often have the gumption to finish their projects, unless they happened upon one by chance at some point later and were seized by the moment to pick it up and begin anew. In that sense, they recreated themselves every day. And in that manner, piece by piece, through alternate periods of intense play and intense sleep, they were able to produce masterworks of technology: computers, and tracking and communications devices, and vehicles that could withstand the rigors of space travel. And they parked one of these vehicles behind the dark side of the moon, loaded with sophisticated radio and recording equipment so powerful they were able to beam signals directly through the moon, and so in secret monitored the goings-on on earth and the treatment of cats there. Their equipment was so far ahead of anything mere humans had developed to that point; they tracked not only activities and actions but also thoughts and feelings, and so distinguished between those things people did out of malice or anger and those things done by accident or through ignorance.

They did this because they were curious, just like the cat part

of them. They were able to do it because they were scientific ge-
niuses, just like the human part of them. And what they did in
response was due to the instinctual, animal part of both their feline
and human sides. They were seized with anger at what they gleaned
and immediately vented it.

Being able to discern who was truly guilty of harming their
brethren on purpose, for thrills or for a feeling of power or simply
because pain gives pleasure to certain minds, the cat people pun-
ished swiftly and severely. There was no ceremony, no premedita-
tion, no ritual. These were instinctual retributions. Malcolm Friday,
who had murdered an entire litter of kittens by running a hose
from the tailpipe of his Chevy S-10 and inserting the free end into
a carefully lidded cardboard box and then turning on the engine
and asphyxiating all twelve beings inside instead of driving them to
the Humane Society only a mile away, was simply hit on the head
with the end of a shovel, caving his skull in.

When the cat people came it wasn't too much of a surprise to
Frank and Eva Florshime, a retired couple (ages respectfully with-
held) in Columbus, Ohio. The Florshimes owned Butch, a power-
fully built neutered tom of undetermined heritage with short wiry
fur and slanted eyes that reminded them of depictions of aliens
they had seen on the covers of scandalous supermarket pulp magazines and in such books as *Communion*. In fact, they often joked to
each other that their cat looked like an alien, the way he would cock
his head and stare at them with his two dark almonds, impossibly
brilliant and intelligent, and the air with which he carried himself,
regal though not yet haughty, as if he knew he were special, royalty
among peasants, but deigned to live among the lower class because
he happened to like these particular two members of it. So they
left their front window open even at night in winter to allow their
alien eunuch king free access to and from his domicile, and fed
him the best cat food they could find and choice scraps from their
own meals, never just the fatty leftover trimmings from a steak or

fish, or greasy drippings from a chicken or pork dish. And the cat people looked down from behind the moon and saw that Butch's couple treated him so respectfully, with so much more devotion than fealty required, that when they landed their vehicle directly on the Florshimes' front lawn, leaving a circular burn mark that mimicked those the *Weekly World News* had trumpeted across its pages only a week before, the ones proclaimed to have been left in a wheat field on Salisbury Plain in Wiltshire, England, as irrefutable proof that Stonehenge had been built by aliens, the cat people ushered the Florshimes into their vehicle with eyes gleaming and sat them upon a makeshift throne and placed a garland of catnip around each one's head and a golden scepter in each one's hands and ordained them both ministers in the ruling cabinet. Butch was awarded title to the entire 160 acres that comprised Fox Run, the subdivision the Florshimes had, until then, lived in and that despite its name hadn't seen a fox in more than a century but was flush with birds, rabbits, squirrels, and other small rodents that Butch loved, and every household in the subdivision was commanded to leave the front windows open twenty-four hours a day with no restrictions put on hunting if you were a cat.

Then there was the case of Alice Meechum, a thirty-year-old college writing instructor. She owned a beautiful tom she had found caterwauling uncontrollably under her red Dodge Caliber during her move from Wilkes-Barre, Pennsylvania, to Chico, California. The noisy thing proved to be pathetically puny despite its booming voice, perhaps aided by the amplifying effect of the vehicle's metallic undercarriage, and she had taken pity on him and brought him with her with the intention of dropping him off at the animal shelter once she arrived in her new home city. However, she fell in love with the creature on the ride there, smitten by the way he curled up to sleep on her shoulder as if she were a pirate and he a parrot. And once moved into their new apartment, the cat, named Ernest Joyce Thomas Woolf Mann Stein after various modernist writers but called Ernie for short, took splendidly to the fresh environs, running about the waxed wooden floors and sliding onto his face because his claws hadn't grown enough yet, climbing the screens of the windows that stretched nearly from floor to ceiling in the heavily partitioned Victorian home, until Alice trained him to desist by squirting water at him from a plastic plant spray bottle, and crawling under the dusty '55 Plymouth coup in the old garage out back, either something of a regression or a tribute to his earliest days, the feline equivalent of wrapping up in a childhood blanket.

But there were mischievous things Alice did to the cat, like tying rubber bands to his tail just to watch him spin in circles until he fell over in his desperation to rip off the unnatural appendages, or painting a broad magenta stripe down his back to make him look like a skunk when she rinsed a henna product into her hair, or allowing him to lick out the sticky insides of a pint carton of hippie ice cream—banana spelt crunch was her favorite—because she knew that in his fervor to get the goodies he would insert his entire head into the carton and it would become stuck thereupon, and, uncertain as to exactly what had transpired, he would take the natural prescriptive measure of doing the opposite of what had gotten him into the mess in the first place, which was moving forward into it, and so would try in vain to back out of it rather than claw at it, much to the laughter of Alice. They were harmless pranks, and ones that never put Ernie in physical danger, but they annoyed the cat people, and Alice was made to walk the chain gang of like tormentors when the cat people formed their communal work details, putting a garden trowel in her hands and forcing her to march for two years shackled at the ankles to two others who, under the watchful eye of cat people wearing wide-brimmed cowboy hats and brandishing shotguns, followed the band of roving cats they were assigned to, digging up the earth whenever one had to relieve him- or herself and then filling the hole back up so that the cats would never have to dirty their own paws.

Joe Flannery, age thirty-seven, a short, plump welder in a machine shop in the north end of Spokane, Washington, was disemboweled and his guts strung out over High Bridge like some macabre kite that never got off the ground, and the rest of his body was left open like a cavernous pussing ulcer exploded on the skin of the concrete shoulder abutment that kept the other motorists, the good ones, the ones the cat people still allowed to drive cars, from falling over the edge, and provided an example for the in-between ones, those who had heard the mewling of sad lost kittens calling piteously from the depths of a garbage dumpster or the forlorn edge of a road in a soaking wet cardboard box and yet had failed to stop and do anything about it, thinking someone else would come along to provide a better home for those wayward souls. Flannery had been one of those who had abandoned a litter of kittens after their mother had made the mistake of taking up with the cat equivalent of a drunken sailor visiting from another port; after a short and sordid romance, the wily mate had knocked up his mistress and left her high and dry while he lit out for exotic destinations unknown. And so Flannery took it upon himself to tightly duct tape each of the seven newborns who had survived their jarring eruption from the warm salty sea of their mother's womb and into the cold hardness of the world, and he had stacked his terrified rolls like duct-taped-colored apples in a crate and left them in the bushes. The cat people, having no ironic sense, didn't wrap him tightly in duct tape like low-tech butchers making an experimental sausage, or even throw him into some bushes, say a thick stand of wild roses or a patch of nettles. Outraged, they just took him for a ride and gutted him and threw him out the window when they were done, and he sat on the edge of High Bridge until the insects came and chewed him out and the sun dried him up and the wind finally blew him over the edge, sending his leathery corpse hurtling toward rocky Latah Creek with his intestines, snagged in a crack in the cement above, trailing behind him like a bungee cord.

And so in that manner, the cat people judged and wreaked their vengeance.

THE GREAT SILVER CACTUS OF DRIGGS, IDAHO

Munching on a sourdough-and-raisin biscuit at Cody's Cafe, in the little ski town of Driggs, Idaho, somewhere near the Wyoming border, you open your Rand McNally & Company Road Atlas to see exactly where you are, and that's smack in the middle of section K-9. You marvel at the synchronicity, for Cody is a shepherd mix of half-undetermined heritage, and it's his cafe. He has free roam of the place, so he roams freely between the tables as if to make sure everything's hunky-dory, and if it isn't, he gives his tail a shake and nobody cares if there are pits in the fresh-squeezed orange juice. It's a strange place for a carnivore like Cody, you muse, considering the mostly vegetarian menu.

On the table, a crescent of seeds slowly waxes while you sip your juice and look out the window. Driggs is backed against the Teton Range, and you can't help thinking that "Teton" reminds you of "titty hard-on." *Pig*, you hear a voice say—you're not quite sure whose—but there they are: a chorus line of unbridled breasts aroused by the touch of white clouds, the mother of them all, the Grand Teton, rising (according to your trusty Rand McNally) 13,771 feet high exactly due east. If you shot an arrow from Driggs and aimed it over that well-stacked Grand Dame it would, provided your aim was true and perhaps with the aid of a good westerly, sail between the forty-third and forty-fourth parallels and land directly (you flip the pages back and forth several times to discern this) in Mount Pleasant, Michigan, which is where you're from and the city you're running from, since the woman who once owned the silver Celtic cross lives there. You're in Driggs, Idaho, and she's not even on the same page, you think before snapping the atlas shut and returning to your juice and Stonehenge of seeds.

In the northern woods of your home state stands a peculiar spectacle called the Cross of the Woods. It's actually a crucifix, three stories high, Jesus' punctured extremities dripping an imaginary sylvan waterfall over pilgrims thirsty for blood. You had been fascinated by the concept, and though you're a whimsical agnostic, your quest to behold the sight of a towering icon bleeding in the middle of a forest actually took on something of a religious nature. But once you walked back along the trail to the clearing and looked up to see those luminous white feet nailed over you, you couldn't bear to look up anymore. It reminded you of the father who had ditched you while you were still in diapers, left you hanging just like that poor savior. Sometimes kitsch is best on a smaller scale, you decided, on a level with toy poodles and Andrew Lloyd Webber recordings—tasteless but innocuous. That monstrosity actually made you feel guilty: about yet another fight with your then-girlfriend over commitment, putting down toy poodles, leaving the toilet seat up, your dad leaving, everything, like it was all your fault. Or was that the whole point? You turned and walked out of that clearing and never beheld the beatific face of what at the least was probably an impressive sculptural feat.

Cody sashays by you then (an old dog, his presumably brittle hips give him a rather sensual gait), and you break from your thoughts to bend over and pat him on the head, slipping him part of your breakfast. *You're teaching him bad habits.* That was definitely your ex-girlfriend. She's a witch. She liked to tell you she was a good witch, like Glinda in *The Wizard of Oz,* someone surrounded by an aura of happy pink bubbles and smiles, but she owned a temper like a cyclone, and you still aren't convinced she won't drop a house on you. She probably did put a hex on you, but fortunately, you don't believe in hexes—like your belief in God, also subject to sudden change.

Until the breakup, it had been worth dodging her chanting because of the passion, and that's why the mountains look like supine, prehistoric Venuses. They aren't full from the crush of menstrual blood, however, but from lack of it. She had been a month late when you last saw her three months ago, and while that wasn't entirely unusual—she was irregular in everything she did—the thought that you may have left something behind besides your fleece-lined mad bomber jacket had chilled you even more than the weather. It had been a fine September moseying through Indiana, Illinois, and Wisconsin, and even a dandy October through Minnesota, South Dakota, and Wyoming, but it's now late November in Idaho, and you're broke. Your car had been packed for you in a hurry, leaving you bereft of most of your possessions, but in the bustle of eviction, she had lost one of the many pieces of fine jewelry she wore; that night while undressing in your motel room, you discovered the silver cross in the pocket of your blue plaid flannel shirt. Your first thought was to flush it down the toilet, a symbolic if tardy act of defiance, but a closer inspection of its intricately braided etchings—and a heft of its substantial weight—convinced you to hang onto it. The man at the antique shop you visited the next day offered you three hundred dollars on the spot, so you guessed it was worth many times more. If worse came to worst, you decided, at least you had a small nest egg, the means to start a fresh new life—maybe not that suggested by a cross, paganized or not, but you would take life where you found it.

Draining your juice, you stand to leave, and that's when you notice the string with the unraveled granny knot at your feet. You squat and furiously scan the floor, under the table, only to find an irregular patch of sourdough crumbs—grisly remains, you suddenly realize, which Cody's great pink tongue had so frantically sought that he must have lapped up the flash of silver lost in spatters of saliva. Your canine host ate your Celtic cross.

You slowly sit back down. When the waitress walks by, you order a water and, as a smoke screen, ask to see the menu again. You have no other choice but to wait and allow beneficent nature the care and delivery of your nest egg in its due time.

At first, you don't see it, for the moon's full brightness makes the shadows around your ankles even blacker, but then the wind blows a scrap of brush away, and it's revealed: in a shiny black pile of shit. Something told you it was there. Maybe the vibration of it simply tickled your subconscious, which lately has seemed to enjoy masquerading as an outside influence. That's what you try to tell yourself, anyway.

You step lightly around the pile and ponder it. *What is love?* you think. Is it something physical, that can form itself into a seed and swim into the belly of a woman? Or is it an essence, like silver, not the silver itself but its color: ethereal, shimmering, something that can be seen, even felt, but not grasped with fingers? Or is it both, a concept and a living thing that grows, that needs to be fertilized and nurtured? These thoughts disappear when you recognize raisins from the biscuit Cody had beamed—as if he controlled a transporter from *Star Trek*—directly from your hand and into his stomach, he ate it so quickly. It reminds you of an old episode of that show, the original series, in which a witch shrinks the Enterprise down to the size of a pendant, transforming the ship into a gift to be worn around someone's neck.

You remember going Christmas shopping with your witch at Bronner's in Frankenmuth, Michigan, which proclaims itself all up and down I-75 as being the world's largest Christmas store. For a pagan, she celebrated Christmas with a zeal becoming of most Christians and retailers, and as a cat person, she bought anything picturing, poeticizing, or otherwise relating to cats. You always thought that for someone who claimed to be an individual, it was awfully stereotypical to be a witch with a cat as a familiar.

She was also quite the amateur herbalist. From her you learned that young cattail pollen can be made into an all-purpose flour; that violets not only purify the blood, they're tasty in jams or salads; and that sage tea is good for delayed menses. But whenever she ground her pungent seeds with her mortar and pestle, you suspected it made you grind your teeth at night. She liked to talk about the three-fold rule: anything she did to another, whether good or bad, would come back to her, only three times better or worse, so it made sense to cast only good spells; that made sense to you, too, so you couldn't understand why she didn't seem to follow her own rule—after all, it wasn't the three-fold *suggestion*, it was a *rule*. It sounded very proper and ethical, a karmic version of the old Golden Rule cloaked in herbs and incense, but she always did these things to you that you knew she wouldn't like done to her, like throwing you out of the house in the rain at three in the morning. But that was three months ago, and you only hope she's been thrown out of *three* houses in three wet, early mornings since.

So there it sits, shining still—the dung hasn't dulled it—and you reach for a stick to poke the cross out with. But there aren't any sticks nearby, and you walk a few paces away before realizing your pile is nearly indistinguishable from all the others around it and from the scattered stones and deceptive black shadows of the field behind Cody's; had you not been overcome with the sense of having nearly stepped in it, you wouldn't even know where it is now, and your whimsy births a nascent faith in a capitalized Fate.

As you bend over to pick the cross out gingerly with your fingers, it moves. You pull your hand back, not wanting to get bitten by whatever bug might have spawned in the shit, but the cross comes at you anyway, as if it wants to be caught. You step back then and watch as the twisted silver braids continue to bloom and grow: buds form, swell, and open, flowers burst with seed, and the cross reaches for the mountains on the black horizon, then the sky. But something about it changes. You watch as tiny silver spines break out all over its plumping flesh, and the horizontal bar bends upward at either end like a referee signaling a touchdown, and the base becomes even stouter and roots itself into the ground. It shoots up to the height of three stories, and with the moonlight shimmering off its silver surface, it appears to glow. Your cross has just grown into a giant cactus.

Television camera crews and newspaper and radio reporters surround you the next morning as you explain the entire story, from Cody's on, anyway.

Didn't it hurt carrying a cactus in your pocket?

It wasn't a cactus, it was a cross. It grew into a cactus.

Are you an experimental botanist?

No, but you've heard of Mendel, you watch *Victory Garden* on P.B.S., and when you were young, you worked for a truck farmer, picking snow peas for fifteen cents a quart basket.

What of reports of Virgin Mary sightings in nearby Tetonia?

The name reminds you of "titty on ya," and you think of medieval paintings of the Virgin feeding her newborn in which her breasts spring out of the most unlikely places, directly from her collarbone in one rendition, evidently the artists' collective way of showing that Mary was no ordinary woman and thus ensuring her deification despite the nudity—but you only say you're sure it's an unrelated miracle.

They say you can see the face of Jesus on the main hump of the cactus if you look at it from the proper angle in southern light.

Who is "they" anyway?

You suspect the woman who confronted you is part of that enigmatic group. She had been out walking when she saw you in the field behind the cafe, called there after Cody put up an intense howling that repeated shushes and a reminder of the treat you fed him earlier couldn't soothe. Evidently the light of the moon shining off the cactus had been enough to wake him, and enough to make her think aliens had landed. It took you some time to assure her *you* weren't an alien and the cactus wasn't a spaceship. She called the local paper with the news, and it wasn't long before every media hound in the region sniffed it out. Even the most cynical among them couldn't discount the great silver reality behind you, especially since it made a beautiful backdrop for the noon teaser on the local stations.

While you're answering their questions, the cactus bucks spasmodically, and the woman relates a story about a friend who dug up a small, wild member of the *Cactaceae* family and took it home. That plant began doing exactly what yours is now, swaying and shimmying as if to music, and when her friend called a local greenhouse to ask about the mysterious behavior, the man there told her to remove the exotic dancer at once. Shortly after being set down outside, the cactus gave one final, terrific shiver and spilled scores of tiny scorpions to the ground.

As the woman finishes her story, a bright red flower sprouts from the middle of your cactus, and its two great arms drop and join just under the flower so that the entire plant looks like a giant silver Buddha. When the flower opens, you hear a faint cry. The cactus is cradling something in its gentle arms, and, as the wind suddenly kicks up and swirls around you, it bends forward and hands you a squirming little bundle.

It's a boy! a reporter exclaims into a microphone, and an insurance salesman from Boise passes out cigars while the media presses in closer to your beaming but confused face and Cody barks and wags his tail like he's a puppy again. A childless computer consultant slips him a jelly doughnut filled, a sly moment before, with a silver wedding band in the fervent hope that the high desert has suddenly become fertile ground for silver cacti. Cody eats it without chewing, then part of a ham sandwich, then half a pita, then a rolled-over piece of roast beef. *Good boy*, somebody says.

I just waited to see it on the news, your ex-Glinda explains in a letter you receive by next-day air, miraculously, the next day. *Then I knew where to find you. Good luck with social services!* The letter tells all: It wasn't nice of you to leave her with your child (yes, she knew she was pregnant before she threw you out; that's partly what inspired the outburst). Adoption would do no good, it wouldn't serve as revenge, and why should she have to pay for an abortion? You can't believe even she could be so callous, and then the next sentence explains it: she knew that whenever she looked at the child, she would see you, and as bad as she felt, she couldn't stand that thought. You would never commit, but she could take control of the situation and make you face it. So she inserted a wooden Celtic cross into her vagina and pushed it along with her thoughts until it bumped up against the little sperm and egg sleeping together in her uterus; the essence of the child slipped into the cross, and when she pushed it out later, it was pure silver. Then she buttoned the baby into the pocket of your favorite shirt, where you carried him like a surrogate mother. She even included an early Christmas present with her letter, a pair of soft red and green baby booties with matching red and green pajamas embroidered with kittens wearing Santa hats—*from Bronner's*, she wrote. *Meowy Christmas and a Happy New Life!*

You look at your son. As his mother presaged, he sports your thin lips and sharp nose, the same prickly twinkle in his eyes. He's going to be trouble. But when you lift him high above your head, his arms wide in flight, his legs churning, trying to pedal air— the red booty slipping to the floor—you feel the incredible trust in his tiny body, the laughter rolling from his chubby belly, and something, something inside, tells you it's time to stop running.

You place him in the baby carrier next to you, give Cody a scratch behind the ears, and push away the empty bowl on the table. You imagine her now, smugly reposed, enjoying a cattail biscuit with violet jam and a cup of sage tea. You only hope that somewhere down the road, somewhere in the woods between lakes Huron and Michigan, when the moon is high and the tides full, her own water will swell and her face crest in pain with the birth of the three plump cactus berries you'd topped with cactus milk and ate and will bury tomorrow in a steaming pile in the Targhee National Forest just outside of Driggs.

WING WALKING

The first thing you should know is if your bags went to Jackson Hole when you were going to Jacksonville, it wasn't my fault. Whenever somebody finds out what I do, they always have a story about how this went here or that went there. I don't want to hear about it. I've already heard them all. It's not my job to tag the suckers; I just stuff them in the cargo hold. I get paid six-fucking-fifty an hour to do it, but it sure beats sitting behind a desk all day.

Anything you can load on a plane, I load—luggage, of course, plus the mail, live animals, frozen blood, musical instruments, medical samples, hazardous waste, golf bags (the worst, impossible to stack)—*anything*, which is also what people pack into their bags. I don't travel much, but when I do I might be gone for a week and live out of one suitcase. Some people travel across the state—you can see from the tags that they're only going to Pasco or Seattle—and they pack their whole lives with them. A few that come back weigh a good hundred pounds or more. You can tell these right away by how they literally bulge at the seams and don't shiver as they move down the conveyor. Smack one on the sides and it's hard as rock. It's like anything, even the porous limestone of clothing, can become marble if enough pressure is applied.

You've heard of spontaneous human combustion, where people ignite out of the blue? There's also spontaneous bag eruption. Those compacted ones are practically spring-loaded. It doesn't take much—a zipper caught in the conveyor, for instance—to set them off. Then what are you going to do? You just try to stuff everything back inside and load it on the plane. We haven't had a late takeoff due to ramp service for almost two years now, and we're not going to let some joker's poor packing screw it up.

I like this work, though, which is why I want to stay in the business. It's real. Where else can you actually be down on the ground with the big planes? We don't get the *really* big planes here. The airport's too small—don't let the "International" fool you. The only reason it's international is because one of the other airlines has a flight into Canada. So we don't get the 747s or 767s, or even the MD-11s. But depending on the model, the 727s and 737s can sport wingspans of a hundred feet or more.

This is going to sound corny—I don't even know why I'm telling you—but there's something about these planes. There's a power to them, and I kind of soak it up when I'm near them. I get this feeling in my chest like it's expanding, and I'm not talking about breathing. It's like I can see my heart out there on the ramp, so big and pulsing almost.

My old man says the fact I don't get my ass back in college shows I'm not as smart as he thought I was. Part of him wants me to have an easier life than he's had, pouring aluminum all day in a foundry for Kaiser, especially now that he's locked out of his job, though he didn't mind it so much back when Henry Kaiser actually owned the place.

"They're all S.O.B.'s," he liked to say about management, "but he's a classy S.O.B."

When the business was sold and started dying, I started calling the new owner The Kaiser.

"What's that supposed to mean?" my old man asked.

I explained that despite a lot of sunny promises, the last kaiser, Wilhelm II, led Germany into the destruction of World War I and was later exiled, like certain people today should be. See?

"You're too damn smart," my old man said. "He's just a piece of shit."

So he'd like to see me rise above the shit and become a classy S.O.B., but I think part of him's secretly proud I'm a working stiff like him. The thing is, I'm with the only airline in this entire airport that isn't union, so I make half of what the other ramp agents do for the same work, and without any bennies. That's not using your fucking head, is what my old man would say about that. So I don't tell him. I let him think I'm out here making gravy.

I got to work at five-fifteen, drag-ass and a little cotton-mouthed, but on time. Joe wasn't around. I waited for about five minutes, but when the ramp started to look fuzzy, I hooked up a couple of carts to a tug and went to pick up the mail by myself—a typical start to the day. Sometimes Joe will eventually sidle into the airport post office to help, but Mondays are usually light, and Griz, our shift leader, comes in late, too, so old Joe must not have felt any compunction or charity. That's okay, because the weather is great in the summer, and I enjoy mornings more by myself. The sky is a blueberry color at first with orange peeling around the edges, and then the sun comes pouring over the mountains. The air is warm enough that you can take off your jacket if you're not tearing around in a tug, but not so blistering as later in the day, when the ramp heats up and the jets send wavering streams of heat all over the taxiways and runways.

Today, though, there was a ton of mail, literally. For some

reason, we had all these packages going to Newark, so it was almost six before I got to the bag room. As usual, everyone was just standing around and bullshitting: Joe, Griz, Devon, and Erika. The two women actually look good in civilian clothing, but you would never know in our uniforms. The crews of other airlines—union airlines—can wear shorts, but we can't, just blue polyester trousers and striped work shirts for us. We look like a horde of Mr. Goodwrenches.

"I got the mail, Griz," I said, looking over at Joe. He held my stare just as steady as I gave it out.

"My hero," Griz said, picking up the clipboard with the baggage manifest on it. Even when he's in a good mood, it's hard to read him. He's got this red face, bristly red mustache and crew cut, and forearms that always look sunburned or windburned depending on the season—a straight flush, except that his arm hairs have a greenish tinge to them. Griz is short for Grizzly Adams. His real name is Dan Hagarty, just like the guy on the old TV show, though he spells it differently. Still. "How much?" he asked.

"I realize it took me awhile," I said. "Who else was the early in today, anyway?"

"Why do you have to act like such a martyr?" Joe said. "It's just the mail, for Chrissake."

"Yeah, well, there was a lot of it today. I could've used some help."

"How *much*?" Griz repeated, tapping the clipboard.

I turned toward him. "At least two thousand."

"On a Monday?"

"See for yourself," I said, pointing to where I'd parked the carts outside the bag room. We don't actually weigh anything but guess, using the formula that one cart packed top to bottom equals a thousand pounds. Our guesses need to be fairly accurate—the pilots base their take-off calculations on how much they're carrying.

It's doubtful a few hundred pounds either way would bring a plane down, but no one wants to test the theory.

Griz waved away my invitation and scribbled the amount with a No. 2 Eagle, which looked like one of those stubby library pencils in his hand. He's a pretty big guy, but his size is more of the I'm-a-little-teapot variety—short and stout. The thing that's spooky about him is that his old man bought the farm in Vietnam, right at the end of the war when Griz was only three, and I think it wigged him out.

"Close enough for government work," he said. Joe turned around and in a minute was kicking and shaking the Coke machine trying to score a free Coke.

We hustled our tails out to load the mail, and by the time we got back, things had picked up in the bag room. The six-fifty flight is usually pretty full because people like to get a jump on their travel, and today was no exception; the conveyor started kicking out more and more bags as the line of bleary-eyed passengers at the ticket counter grew longer and longer. When this happens, you get into a rhythm: check the tags, call out the destinations, lift the bags, sling them into the carts. Check, call, lift, sling. It's not surgery. It's more like being a short-order grill cook. To make unloading easier down the line, we log everything in and separate it out as to whether it's regular, hot, local, or a carrier bag for another airline. In case we forget how to do it, there's a subtle reminder on the wall above our heads:

Read the tag, load the bag
So easy it's scary

On the sign, there's a little picture of a black bat. He's part of the Baggage Action Team. Get it? It's amazing how some guys don't, like Joe, for example—if he's even pitching bags at all. You never saw a guy who has to go to the bathroom so much, or bullshit with security up front, or take a smoke break, even though he's practically the only one here who doesn't smoke—whatever he's doing, he doesn't do it in the bag room. It's not like this is terribly hard work. Sure, it gets a little hectic when it's close to take-off time and all the last-minute arrivals arrive, but even then it's just a matter of doing what that little bat says.

Joe and I have known each other for years, all the way back to high school, when I was a big shy kid and he seemed pretty clever because he knew baseball as well as physics. It took me awhile, but I eventually figured out he was a fake. We actually hung out all the way through his first year of college, my sophomore year, before he stopped wanting to sneak into the bars and party on the weekend. Next thing I knew he had married Sue, his high school girlfriend, and suddenly none of my girlfriends were good enough to double-date with. He seemed to feel he was way above my whole scene.

Because I have this long hair, these John Lennon glasses, and more schooling than most everyone else, they all call me Prof. I'm only a year away from graduating if I want, but I never told my old man that. I also never told him my scholarship ran out after two years, and that I'd paid for everything with student loans after that. He thought school was great as long as it was on the government's dime, but he'd want to smack me up good if he knew I spent my own cash on it, came that close to finishing, and didn't.

In school I studied philosophy at first before switching to history. I liked that stuff; I just couldn't figure out how to make it relate to real life. What was I going to do, be a teacher? I couldn't stand the thought of going through all that education just to make less money than my old man—back when he was working, that is. He would think I'm a world-class idiot for sure. So then I switched to journalism, until I learned how much those guys make. Isn't a college degree supposed to be worth something?

Anyway, who wants to sit on his ass all day like an editor or an academic? With college, my first mistake was not taking time off right after high school. I had that scholarship dangling in front of me, but if I had really been smart, I would have gotten some life experience first. It's easy to see what a dumb-ass you were when you get some distance. That's what going away to college should have done, which was my second mistake: I didn't go far enough. I went to my hometown school. I knew everybody.

I know something now that I'm almost twenty-three that I didn't when I was eighteen, and I'm not going to make another mistake by wasting my time and money in school. Like I said, I'm hardly busting the bank yet, but I've got a plan. They're always looking for smart people in this business, so after I get a little more experience, and as soon as there's an opening at another airline—a union airline, with flight bennies and everything—I'm out of here. Then I'll be going somewhere for sure.

So Griz was marking down bags when he bent over and peered at one, at its zipper—the actual part you pull, with the brand name on it and a hole in one end so that it looks like a tiny key. He held it between his fingers, rubbing it, and then in one motion picked up a bag in each hand, turned, and flung them into the front cart seven or eight feet away. From the sound they made, they must have weighed forty pounds each.

"Damn!" he said.

"Not what you're looking for, eh Griz?" I said.

"It *is* what I'm looking for. It's the elusive obsidian seahorse."

Griz collects zipper pulls. He's got a whole fishbowl of them at home, a five-gallon job, but he wears the Atlantics on a chain like a necklace. Atlantic is the brand with a seahorse for its logo; it's on all of their zippers, but it's slightly different depending on the style of the suitcase and the year it was made. Griz has a bounty out on these creatures. Not just any one—Atlantic is a popular brand—but in particular those with variously colored oval backgrounds set into them. He's got ten dollars for anyone who finds a chocolate, emerald, or purple one. For the "elusive obsidian seahorse," he'll pay twenty.

"Oh yeah?" Erika said, interested in the conversation for the first time. Tall and muscular, like a triathlete, she only works here summers now; the rest of the year she's a mechanic at an airstrip in Antarctica. She walked over to the leaning tower of luggage in the front cart and was about to give the zipper pull Griz had examined a good yank when he wagged his finger and said, "Uh, uh. You know the rules."

He knows how the crew is around here. Ten bucks can get you pretty drunk if you spend it right, and twenty will keep you busy at a casino for a while. Everyone is normally pretty cool about other people's stuff, but where there's a free night of shots and slots involved, they lose all sense of morality, yanking on zipper pulls, running them into the ends of belt loaders. Griz won't take any of those. Poaching, he calls it.

"I lost about twenty bucks on Saturday," Erika said. "I need to bankroll myself again."

"I don't care what you do when you're out roamin' the wild savannah," Griz said. "But don't even *think* about poaching on my watch."

Even in their natural state, bags are constantly getting snagged on something: the conveyor in the bag room, the corners of carts, belt loaders, cargo hold rivets, each other. People would never bother locking their luggage if they knew how easily they pop open all the time. Not only are we always finding zipper pulls, sometimes the zipper itself is attached and often with a lock fastened to the other end, dangling together like some weird charm. We have to pick these up off the ramp because they're F.O.D.—foreign object debris. If sucked into a jet's intake, any piece of scrap, even a button, can dent or twist the turbine blades and cause a plane to go down.

Ingestions, they're called. And it's not just objects that get sucked in. Another sign in the bag room warns: "Fight feathered F.O.D. Stop all bird feeding, intentional or unintentional." In the training video we had to watch, these oddly inert fowls—they must be dead already—shoot down a wind tunnel into whirring turbine blades and disintegrate in puffs of bone and blood. Loose coins, headphones, hats, and other stray articles of clothing can get ripped right off you, or pull you in, too. Over twenty-five people around the world from this airline alone have been killed that way and—almost as important, it seems, from how much it's stressed—caused thousands of dollars of damage to airline equipment. Griz used to wear all the zipper pulls he found until they weighed a couple of pounds; one time, not knowing an engine had been fired up, he walked too near the intake and was nearly pulled in by his necklace. He was lucky. According to our Jet Aircraft Blast and Suction Protection training module, by the time you can feel the suction, it's usually too late.

That's when he decided to wear only Atlantic zipper pulls. For him, I think it's the thrill of the hunt that makes them so valuable. They way they hang there like little trophies, they remind me of those strings of dried ears some guys in 'Nam stitched together.

"Who had lav cart yesterday?" Griz suddenly barked out. He's the shift leader, he knew perfectly well it was me, but for some reason, he wanted to be all theatrical about it.

"Why, you feeling plugged up?" I played along. Back when Griz actually had to do grunt work like cleaning the lavatory cart, he once forgot to wear rubber gloves and got the blue disinfectant on his fingers. Later, he ate some airport chili dogs and ended up with the worst case of incontinence in his life. He always blamed it on the blue stuff, not the chili dogs.

"Why don't you go out and take a close look under gate one, funny guy." He seemed serious, but like I told you, sometimes it's hard to tell. "Go on. We can handle it in here."

So I shrugged and walked out toward where the six-fifty flight was waiting, quiet and empty in the early morning light. Did you know that's when seahorses mate? I once saw a TV special on this. Every day at pre-dawn the seahorse couple meets, intertwining their prehensile tails and practicing synchronized swimming. When the real courtship dance begins, it can last up to eight hours long—the same as a shift here. Only their day ends with the female depositing her eggs into the male's pouch, where he fertilizes them. That's right, the *males* bear the young, as many as a couple thousand at a time. While the guys are knocked up, the females—seamares?—can prepare more eggs. Some stallions can give birth in the morning and be pregnant again by evening. No wonder Griz digs the things.

Anyway, as soon as I got close enough, I realized the fuzzy ramp I'd seen earlier hadn't been my imagination. It was bumpy. And blue. I took calculus in high school. I know how to subtract from the exponent to find the derivative. I walked back to the bag room feeling pretty sheepish, though I covered it up as soon as the guys could see me.

"The night guys are *pissed* at you," Devon said. She should know. She was a night guy who was working that morning so she could have the weekend off. What I'd done was forget to close the lav cart back up after I'd emptied it the day before. All the shitting and pissing that gets done in those cramped little airplane heads, along with everything people flush despite the signs that say not to, ends up in a holding tank that we pump into our lav cart on the ground, which Devon was doing when suddenly this foul sludge went pouring out the bottom and all over the ramp. She caught my mistake pretty fast, but gravity worked faster, leaving them with a stew of toilet paper, shit, cigarettes, swizzle sticks, sanitary napkins, and piss-smelling blue water.

It was a rookie mistake, I admit, but I was a little upset when

Griz told me he'd have to write me up for it.

"Aw, come on, Griz," I said. "The night guys never do any work anyway, none of them except Devon here. I was doing them a favor."

"For Chrissake," Joe decided to butt in, "you're not going to try to get out of this one too, are you?"

"Why's it any of your business?" I said.

"I'm just asking a question," he said. "You know, engaging you in a little Socratic dialogue."

That's the kind of lame shit he's always pulling. I mean, bringing up Socrates to make himself look witty? Griz must have sensed the tension, because he said, "Take it easy. I'm just messing with him."

"Hey, I never should have been written up for that tug incident," I said, worked up pretty good now. "Everyone speeds in those things, and anyway, it was raining, so I couldn't see. They ought to fix that damn wiper."

"We know, we know," Devon piped up. "Or are you gonna give us another dissertation on it, eh Prof?"

"No, man, that was Saturday night," Erika said. "Doctor of drinking. Where do you think I can get a degree like that?"

"You're already halfway there," Devon said.

"What else is a girl to do at the South Pole?" Erika shot back grinning. "I learned how to get by."

"So what about that dissertation?" Joe said.

I *had* been a little wound up when I met Erika and a couple of her friends because I'd visited my old man earlier that day. He was looking rough, but Joe didn't need to know that. "I'm saving it for when I graduate to another airline," I told him.

Some airlines have a reputation for guys riffling through the baggage—have you ever seen that clip on *60 Minutes*?—but we're just the opposite. We put things back into bags. Stuff is always falling out, and not just from exploded bags. People just don't know how to pack. Or else they buy cheap luggage. My old man still uses the J.C. Penny set he and my mom got as a wedding present before he got it in the divorce; the only reason it's lasted this long is because he never goes anywhere. He would freak out if he knew this, but I've become a luggage snob. It's an occupational hazard. Day after day you see what cheap luggage gets you. Birth control pills pop out of a backpack with girl scout badges sewn on it. A porno mag from an expensive golf bag. A hash pipe in the shape of a naked woman from an Army duffel.

Today, it was a bright red teddy.

"Check this out," I said, picking it up off the floor where it had fallen. I modeled the lacy thing against my body; it barely covered my belly button.

"I've got one of those," Erika said.

"You thinking of changing careers?" Griz asked me.

"Are you kidding?" Joe butted in. "He's a lifer. He'll still be here ten years from now, cleaning out the lav cart."

He was finally starting to bother me, the way he was mouthing off in front of Griz. Nobody likes to think they'll stay here because it's non-union and the pay is crap, but Griz has a wife and two kids, and management keeps stringing him along, raising his salary just enough that he can't afford to chuck it all to look for another job. Ever since he got out of high school, he's been working here. He's twenty-eight now but looks ten years older.

"Look who's talking," I said. Sometimes you revert back to that kind of junior high attitude when you're around it all day. "You work here, too, you know."

"You've been here how long—almost three years?" Joe asked.

"What's that supposed to mean?"

"I'm just wondering why you aren't any better off, that's all."

"And what do you know about my life?"

"I know you're not a shift leader yet; anyone can see that.

How come? Why is it you just seem to keep getting passed by?"

"You think you're such hot shit," I said, "but you're not the only one around here with plans." Joe is taking summer classes, as if he doesn't get enough during the regular school year, and after this quarter, he's done; we all know he's leaving after that. Good riddance is my feeling on the whole thing. Good fucking riddance.

Griz made a clucking noise in his throat. "A couple of old hens," he chortled. The bags were starting to back up on the line, and we had to run everything to the plane in a few minutes, so he snatched the teddy from my hands and asked, "Where did it come from?"

We checked the bags on the conveyor, but all of them were locked up tight. No one knew how long the teddy had been lying around, so we checked the bags on top of the piles in the carts, but nothing going there either. Bags were really starting to shoot out from the ticket counter up front, so finally Griz plucked the first one he saw with an outside pocket on it—a Pierre Cardin, all leather—and stuffed the teddy deep inside, zipping it in solid.

"There," he said. "Someone's got a nice surprise waiting for them."

We all headed out to load the plane, with Griz driving the bag train, Erika next to him, and me, Devon, and Joe walking. I kept my eye out for F.O.D. and found three zipper pulls under the front belt loader—a Ricardo, a generic with a lock on it, and an old Travelpro that read "The Original Rollaboard"—but no seahorses.

They're not just hard to find in the watery mirage of the ramp, either. That special I saw said they're dying out because so many have been caught for home aquariums or dried to make souvenirs. But their main use is in traditional medicine, as cures for heart disease, respiratory illnesses, incontinence—and as aphrodisiacs. We're killing an entire genus just so some guys can have hard-ons. I joke with Griz about it sometimes, but stuff like that actually makes me want to disappear, like an extinct animal or human dignity.

Because the first flight is usually so full, a 727, older but larger than a 737, waited for us at gate one. The funny thing is, big as these are on the outside, their cargo holds are tiny, designed in a time when people didn't ship their homes with them when they traveled. I flicked on the belt loader and rode it like an escalator to the cargo hold, bending way over to enter, and waddled to the back all Quasimodo-like while Joe sprawled in the doorway and waited for the bags to start coming. Inside is nothing but sheet metal and molded plastic all the way around, and ramp agents the country over decorate the walls in magic marker, usually hyping their own sexual agility or questioning another's, but often taking sides over whether we should unionize. Most are against it, at least most of those who care to share their artistry. I don't understand these Neolithic wonders who think a near-minimum wage is worth fighting for, although they sometimes include helpful drawings with their rhetoric, such as the one I saw while waiting, of a stick-figure mouth sucking a stick-figure penis above the flourishing caption, "Unions blow!"

When Joe began pitching bags to me, I sat back on my haunches like a catcher to receive them. Some were fastballs—they came shooting at me, like the handbags or luggage with wheels that actually work. Some were knucklers, like the garment bags, flopping all over the place. They come in all different sizes, shapes, and consistencies, and there's only so much room and everything has to fit. When Griz and Erika run the belt loader, they hate to turn that thing off, so the bags kept coming and I kept packing them in as fast and tight as I could without thinking too much about it, even when a hundred-pounder came my way. These are supposed to form the bottom of the stack, but sometimes you've just got to give them a bear hug and jam them in wherever you can.

I was wrestling one of these into position when I heard a grinding followed by silence as the belt loader was turned off. Because I'd had my back turned, I don't know for sure whether Joe intentionally ran that bag into the end of the belt loader, but I swear I saw him pluck that zipper pull like a grape right off the bag as soon as he untangled it.

"Hey Griz!" he yelled, holding up a teardrop shape and grinning his damn head off. "It's pretty dark up here, but this sure looks obsidian to me!" Griz quickly appeared in the doorway and held out his hand. Joe shook his head. "You got twenty bucks?"

"You up here poaching?"

"Me? Griz, you were standing right down there. You saw it was an accident."

"I don't stare at your pretty ass all day." While he said that, he was giving Joe a look like you wouldn't believe, what 'Nam vets call the thousand-yard stare—right through and beyond him a thousand yards, through the cargo hold, its cave paintings, everything. Man, in the right light, those seahorses sure look like dried ears. "What about it, Prof?" he asked, turning to me. "Did we nab ourselves a poacher?"

I looked hard at Joe, but he just gazed back so innocently I wanted to strangle him. Instead, I held out my hands and shrugged. "Hey, I'm actually working here."

Griz turned back to Joe.

"Let me look at it."

Joe shook his head again. "I've got to see cash on the barrelhead, my friend. We can conduct our transaction in the break room." He dropped the zipper pull into his front shirt pocket and buttoned it. Griz disappeared, and pretty soon I was back to my job of somehow making all those odd-shaped packages fit in that little space.

After the plane was loaded, we all stood around and pretended to talk about how we were going to guide it out. They call this a huddle, "Huddle for Excellence." Management and their slogans. We already know what we're going to do, we've done it hundreds of times before, but this way if something goes wrong, we all have our asses covered.

"I'll be marshal," Joe piped up. Always trying to cherry pick.

"Negatory," Erika said. "I've got seniority, and I'm bigger than you, too."

It was already a given Griz was going to run the pushback, even though I'm certified on it as well, because as shift leader he got to choose. Rightfully I could have insisted on being the marshaling agent, but Erika was already giving Joe a good amount of shit, and I actually enjoy wing walking. I slapped her on the shoulder.

"You marshal. I'll wing walk right." I spoke as if Joe wasn't even there.

Wing walking is easy. Someone's on the left, someone on the right. All you've got to do is make sure your wing doesn't bash into anything. Backing up a plane isn't like backing up a car; the pilots don't have rearview mirrors. We're their mirrors. The wing walkers signal any problems to the marshaling agent, who always stays in the pilots' sight in front of the plane's nose. So we're a team, but what I like best is that as a wing walker you're also out there all alone. That much of it is the same as the stunt men and women who actually walk on the wings of looping, rolling biplanes. They're out there in the air with no harnesses on, no safety nets below, nothing except the guts to do it and a sense of freedom I can hardly believe. But sometimes I *can* imagine just a little of what that must be like when I walk alone under the sun beside a monstrous trijet pterodactyl, no sound around me but the whir of turbines like wind in my ears—a big noise, no nit-picky chatter, no asshole trying to make you feel small. In fact, you feel big. You're out there directing this large and fragile instrument with nothing but your own two feet under you, and for a couple of minutes, in the time it takes to move from the passenger gate to the end of the ramp, you have the power to stop everything by bringing both arms together above your head and crossing your bright orange wands in an X.

I put on my reflective safety vest and sunglasses, stuck a couple of earplugs in my ears, a pair of wands in my back pocket, and walked to the pilot's side of the plane in-between the pushback and the right wing. When Griz began backing the plane up, I pulled out the wands and held one in each hand, walking along nice and easy, my left arm hanging free, my right held up to indicate we were clear of all obstructions. The distant mountains waved at me through the jet stream, and the sun glinted off the silver skin of the 727, pure sterling. Even the vapors of hot asphalt rising from below my feet smelled clean.

When the plane was ready to depart the ramp, I chocked its nosewheels to keep from being accidentally run over while I unhooked the tow bar. Then I pulled the bypass pin, giving the power to steer back to the pilots, and after a signal from Erika, unchocked the wheels. She was standing with both arms angled down in the "hold position" signal when I passed her, but I knew that in a few seconds, right before the plane moved into taxi position, she would snap to attention and exchange salutes with the pilot. I don't need any of that. As a wing walker, I can just turn and walk away when my job is done. Behind me, I could hear the plane cranking up its engines. I liked feeling all that heat at my back and knowing I had a long, cool break in front of me.

The only thing is, my break turned into a real pain in the ass. After sending off a flight, the first thing we all do is head for the commissary to wash up. Luggage may look clean, your hands may even appear decent enough, but don't be fooled. Once you give yourself a good scrub, a stream of soapy brown water goes flowing down the drain like the sloughed-off layers of other people's lives.

So I'd just reclaimed my own skin when Joe really started digging under it. He couldn't even wait to get to the break room before unbuttoning his shirt pocket and showing the zipper pull he'd found to Griz. Griz studied it closely and then gave Joe a skeptical look, but I could tell he wanted it.

"So it just got caught, fair and square?" he asked.

"Fair and square," Joe said. The way he said it, so nice and easy, made me tense. I mean, what's fair? Is it watching your old man get locked out of his job only five years from retirement? His hair turning white, his body sagging practically overnight? Is it getting paid six-fucking-fifty an hour to keep proving over and over that you're worth more?

Griz pulled a crisp twenty from his wallet and held it out in a way that gave it a nice crease down the middle.

"Good work, Joe," he said.

Joe carefully folded the bill twice and placed it in a special slot in his wallet. I waited until Griz had gone into the break room before saying anything.

"Nice shortcut to a night on the town," I said. "I saw you pull it off that bag."

"It was already broken," he said. "It was going to fall off anyway."

"You ran it into the end of the belt loader on purpose."

"No, I didn't. And anyway, this isn't for a night on the town. This is going into a joint account with my wife. We've got to save every penny."

"Oh yeah, I forgot. You wouldn't want to have any fun. You and your new life."

Guys like Joe, I wouldn't even give them a second thought if they didn't go around doing things like he did next. He fixed me with this look like I was looking all angry at *him* and said, "You seem pretty uptight about me making a few extra bucks. I'd like to know why you weren't so worried when you lost your scholarship."

"Who says I lost it?" My face felt really hot now. I kind of shook my shoulders just to let some air down my shirt. "It ran out. They do that sometimes, you know."

"Everyone knows where it went. Why do you think they call you Prof?"

"What?" I mean, the guy was plain babbling now. He was just pulling the most random shit out of the air, trying to goad me on for some reason. That's what really got me about it. "I don't even know what you're talking about."

"You're always telling us what a smart guy you are. You figure it out."

"Why are you always riding my ass?"

"Why am *I* riding *your* ass?" he asked instead of answering my question. "You've had it out for me since I started working here." He looked around to make sure no one was listening and then lowered his voice anyway. "You might not believe it, but I was actually worried about you after we stopped hanging out. Then your dad lost his job, and I heard you had really started to—"

"You don't understand how it is," I cut him off. I should have popped him right then, just dropped him to the floor. "You don't understand anything. Things haven't been easy for me lately, but they're coming around. Things are going to turn around any day now."

"That's what you said three years ago." He stared at me like there was something else important on his mind, but all he said was, "We used to be friends."

You know, I've made some mistakes in my life, but I always own up to them. I made three right in a row sending off the one o'clock flight, or I should say three things happened that were mostly my fault. The first was funny, the second stupid, and the third—well, I still don't know what you'd call the third.

I was burning all through the nine-thirty thinking of Joe, and lunch only made it worse, because though I tried to lose myself in *Sports Center* on the airport lounge TV, it wasn't enough to keep my brain occupied. So when the plane from Salt Lake City came in as usual at ten after noon, I wasn't thinking too clearly. I hopped on a belt loader and waited for the Goodwrench Gang to walk the plane in, and as soon as it stopped and its wheels were chocked, I whizzed right into position—in front of a deactivated cargo door. Worse than that, I didn't even know it until I hopped off and tried to open that sucker. Griz was braying like a donkey as I backed up the belt loader and brought it to the right cargo door, and I couldn't help laughing, too. I mean, it was a rookie mistake. That one was pretty easy to shake off. The next one wasn't.

When I jumped off the belt loader again, I opened up the cargo door and climbed right inside without first chocking the wheels. This is a biblical no-no in management's eyes, original sin, the *prima causa* of run-over workers and, like ingestions, thousands of dollars of damage to airline equipment. It doesn't happen often, but it happens, so when our supervisor stepped forward and chocked the wheels himself, I knew I was getting written up for it. Griz must have seen the pissed look on my face because he came up to me after our super had gone off to see about checked bags with the gate agent.

"Sorry, man. You know I got no choice on this one." I nodded and resisted slamming my hand against the inside of the cargo hold. My second write-up in a month. That's the kind of shit that can follow you around and really mess up your plans. "Anyway, get back down here," he said. "We need help with this stiff."

Devon had already wheeled up the flatbed cart to the belt loader. On it was a wooden crate about seven feet long and three feet wide. I told you we load everything, animal, vegetable, and mineral, animate and inanimate. Who knows what happened to this one. Maybe he'd had heart disease; maybe he'd needed a seahorse. Now he was going to Boston, so we were going to pack him in first, all the way in the back. Routine. We'd all done it before. Me, Griz, and Erika held down three corners, and Joe had the other. The stiff must have been part whale, he weighed as much it seems, but that wasn't the problem. I was feeling all wound up about everything—Joe and his bullshit, being written up, the whole lousy day—so my head just wasn't there. I didn't have a good grip on my corner. My hands were all sweaty, and I could feel the thing slipping out of them as we moved from the cart to the belt loader. And then I stepped on a piece of F.O.D. It wasn't too big, probably a zipper pull, but I could feel it through my boot, right in the middle, and it kind of tipped me up—not much, not enough to throw me off balance, but I tried to kick it away for some reason instead of just ignoring it, and I kind of slipped. I did slip. That's when the bulk of this whale came into play, for once I started tipping back just a little and losing my grip even more, he came sloshing at me like a big wave, and everyone else was thrown off balance, too. The whole outfit landed on the belt loader wrong, all off skew, which was still okay; the belt loader wasn't on and wasn't going to crash him into the side of the plane, but I thought I could relax for a minute and catch my breath before we righted that behemoth and sent him on his way. But he must have been settled on there more precariously than I thought because suddenly everyone was yelling, and I had to jump back to keep from getting crushed because that big box was going down.

He was maybe only three feet off the ground, but he hit so hard that not only did the protective wooden crate shatter, the casket lid shook loose. So this thing is sitting there like a shipwreck on rocks, *and his goddamn hand is sticking out*, this horrible, pasty white piece of wax that was somebody's hand. It was bent forward at an odd angle, the fingers all curled up. But the index finger was sticking out a little straighter than the others, and I swear it was pointed at me.

The worst thing about it is that by the time we're loading a plane, passengers are already boarding, and they can see what's going on below. We were huddled close to the fuselage, which makes for a pretty tough angle from the cabin, but that accusing spectacle looked as big as a tail wing to me now, and I was sure anyone staring out the window could see it. But I didn't want to touch the thing. I knew somebody had to do something to cover it up, but I didn't want to touch it. Finally, Griz stepped forward and stuffed it back into place.

"What the hell happened?" he asked, looking around at everyone.

"I don't know," Erika said. "I thought we had it, then all of a sudden I felt it slipping out of my hands."

"Me too," Joe said. "What are we going to do, for Chrissake?"

"Well, we can't load it on the plane like this. Let's get it back on the cart."

Griz shoved the casket lid over until it clunked down tight. The corner that had hit the ramp was splintered, but the other three still looked solid, so we all hunched down and picked it up, this time with Devon on the side to help steady it, and loaded it back onto the flatbed cart. It looked bad sitting there, so even though we'd be shorthanded, Griz had Devon drive it back to cargo. It all happened so fast, no one knew it was my fault.

We loaded up the plane on time, our streak intact, and then went through our usual Bullshit for Excellence. I acted all magnanimous about walking wing, though it's what I wanted, and though we knew we'd catch shit for it later, we all laughed about what had happened.

But when I went to guide that plane out, I didn't feel right. I got this tight feeling in my chest. I couldn't feel the air against my face. Even with my earplugs in, the engines were too loud. As I walked along the right wing, we didn't come close to hitting anything, it was routine, but I practically had to fight myself to keep from bringing my arms up in a bright orange X, from stopping the whole flight, grounding it right there. This time, after I unhooked the tow bar and pulled the bypass pin, I stood on the ramp and watched the plane cruise down the taxiway and onto the runway. And after the others had gone inside to wash up and take a break, I hung around outside for several minutes until I saw the plane take off, make a slow, wide bank overhead, and disappear. I couldn't help thinking it was leaving something behind, and that it was my fault. I couldn't help thinking I was the one who let it go.

ABOUT THE AUTHOR

Image by: Sabina Poole for the Oregon Arts Commission

JEFF FEARNSIDE's short stories have appeared in many literary journals and anthologies, including *Story, Rosebud, The Pinch, Many Mountains Moving, Crab Orchard Review, Bayou Magazine*, and *Everywhere Stories: Short Fiction from a Small Planet* (Press 53). National awards for his writing include a Grand Prize in the Santa Fe Writers Project's Literary Awards Program and the Mary Mackey Short Story Prize, and he is the recipient of a 2015 Individual Artist Fellowship award from the Oregon Arts Commission. His fiction has been nominated for *Best New American Voices* and twice for a Pushcart Prize. He lives with his wife and their two cats in Oregon, where he is at work on a novel.

www.ingramcontent.com/pod-product-compliance
Lightning Source LLC
Chambersburg PA
CBHW030634120726
47904CB00006B/2150